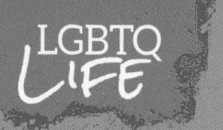

LGBTQ
LIFE

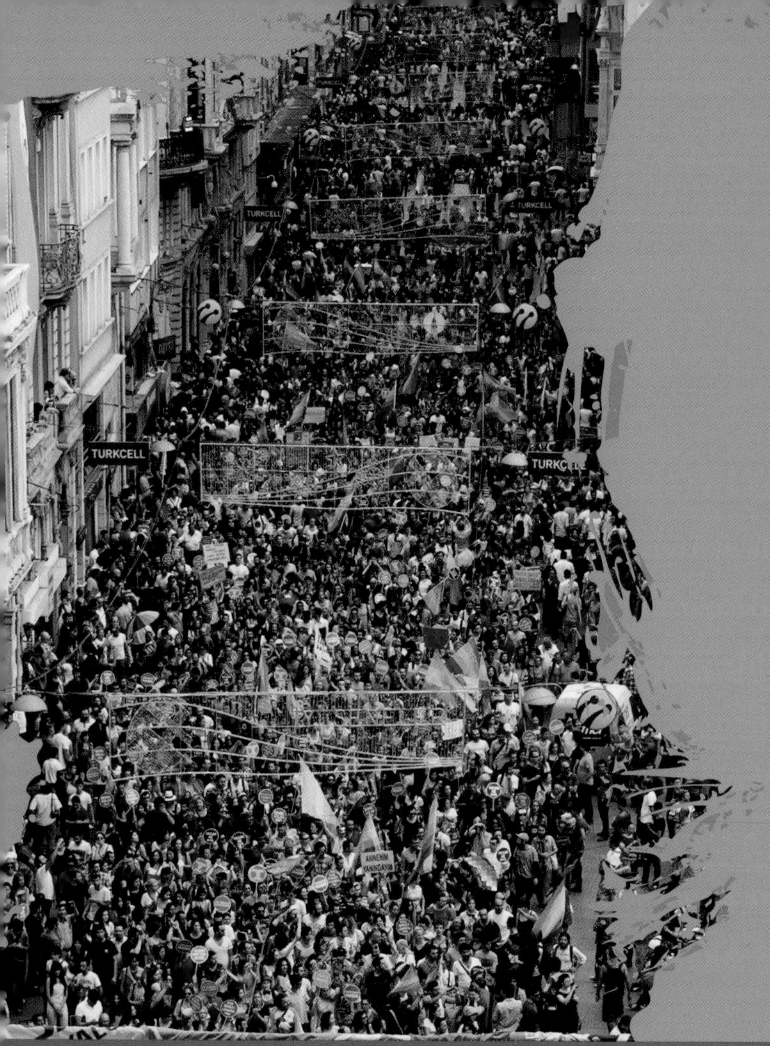

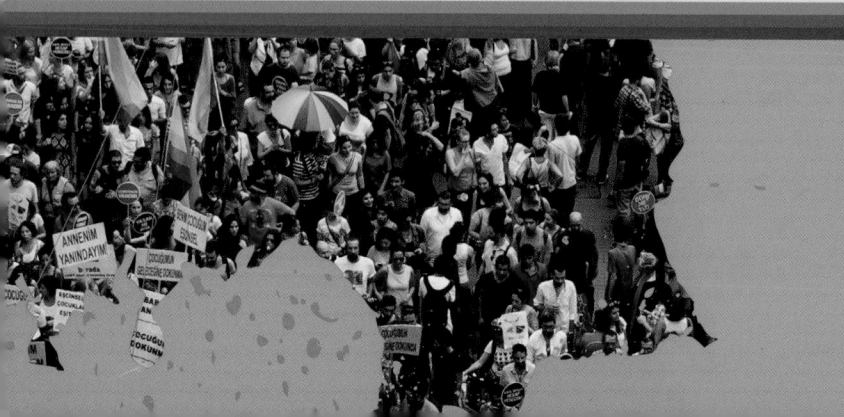

You Are Not Alone
FINDING YOUR LGBTQ
COMMUNITY

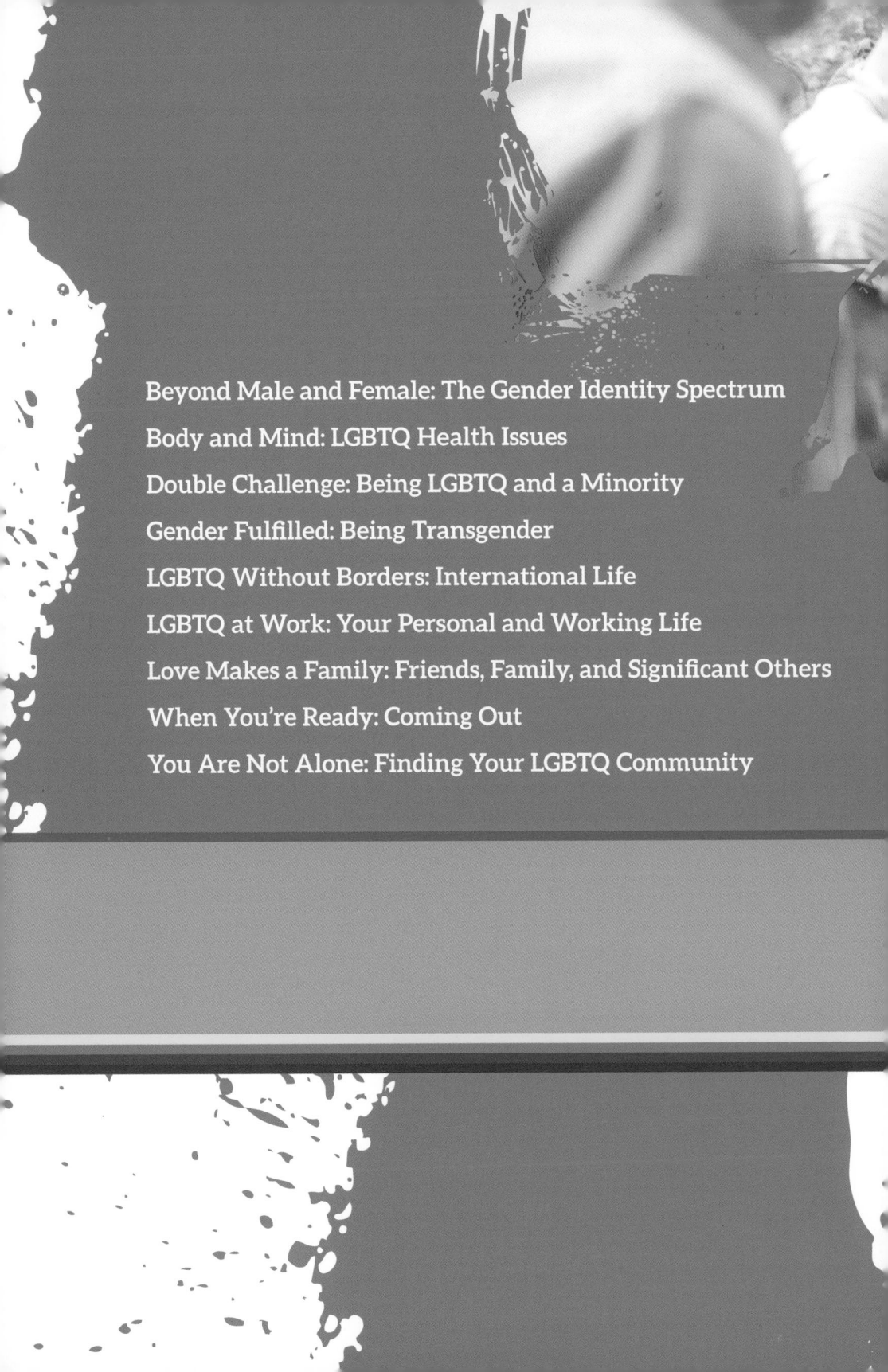

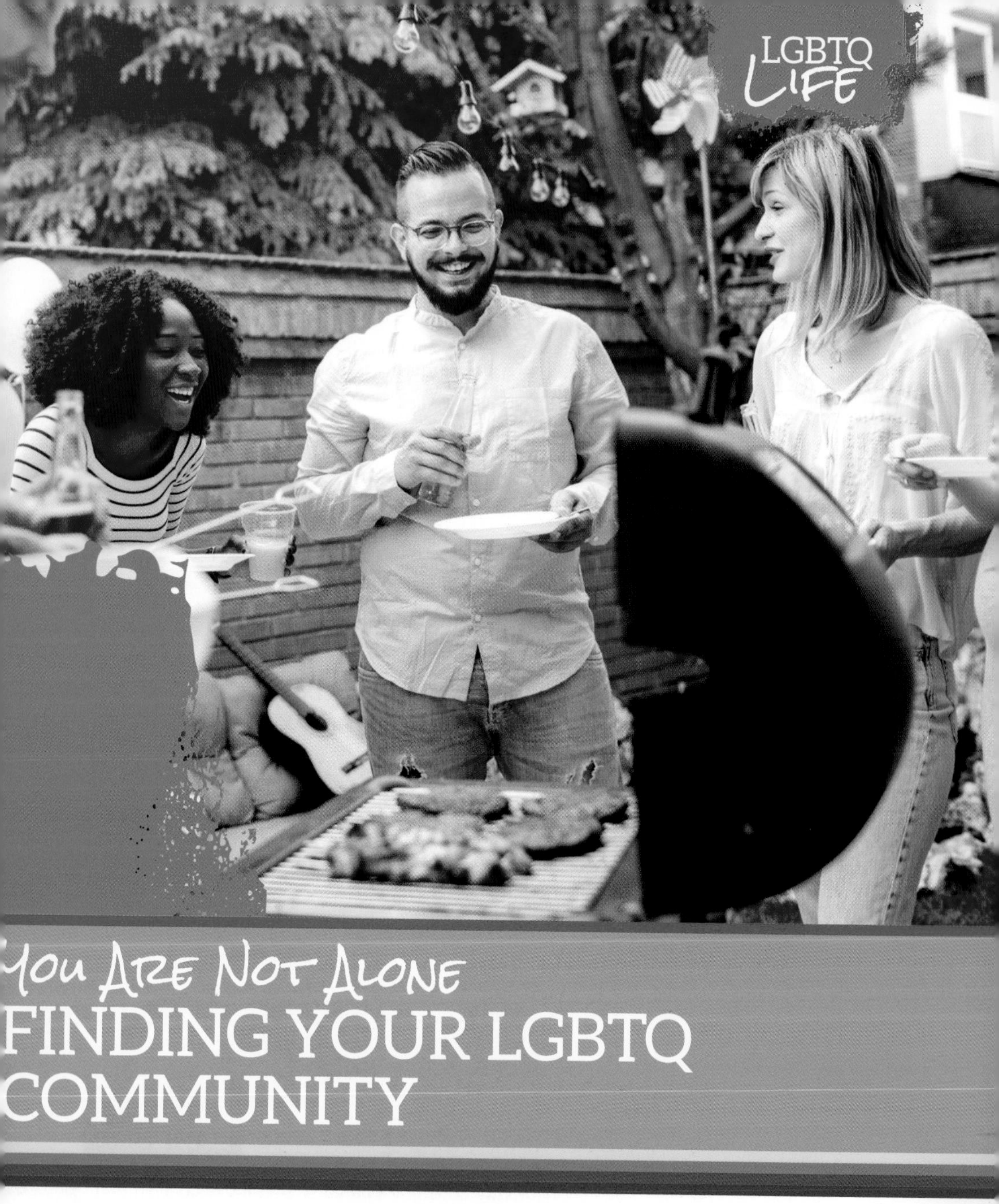

You Are Not Alone
FINDING YOUR LGBTQ
COMMUNITY

By Jeremy Quist

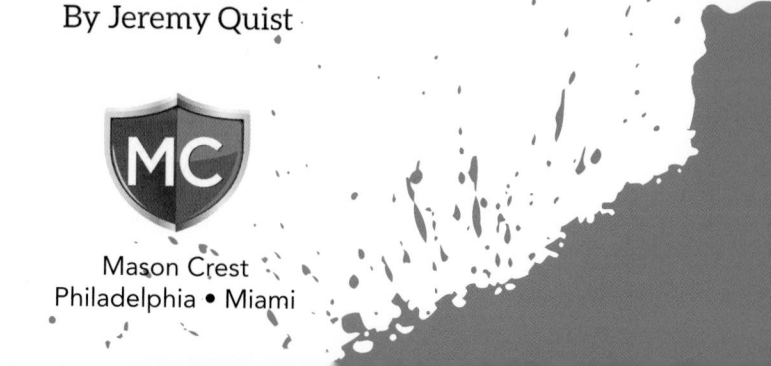

Mason Crest
Philadelphia • Miami

Mason Crest
450 Parkway Drive, Suite D
Broomall, PA 19008
(866) MCP-BOOK (toll free)
www.masoncrest.com

First printing
9 8 7 6 5 4 3 2 1
Series ISBN: 978-1-4222-4273-5
Hardcover ISBN: 978-1-4222-4282-7
E-book ISBN: 978-1-4222-7529-0

Cataloging-in-Publication Data is available on file at the Library of Congress.

Developed and Produced by Print Matters Productions, Inc. (www.printmattersinc.com)

Cover and Interior Design by Tim Palin Creative

QR CODES AND LINKS TO THIRD-PARTY CONTENT

CONTENTS

KEY ICONS TO LOOK FOR

WORDS TO UNDERSTAND: These words, with their easy-to-understand definitions, will increase readers' understanding of the text while building vocabulary skills.

SIDEBARS: This boxed material within the main text allows readers to build knowledge, gain insights, explore possibilities, and broaden their perspectives by weaving together additional information to provide realistic and holistic perspectives.

EDUCATIONAL VIDEOS: Readers can view videos by scanning our QR codes, providing them with additional educational content to supplement the text.

TEXT-DEPENDENT QUESTIONS: These questions send the reader back to the text for more careful attention to the evidence presented there.

RESEARCH PROJECTS: Readers are pointed toward areas of further inquiry connected to each chapter. Suggestions are provided for projects that encourage deeper research and analysis.

SERIES GLOSSARY OF KEY TERMS: This back-of-the-book glossary contains terminology used throughout this series. Words found here increase the reader's ability to read and comprehend higher-level books and articles in this field.

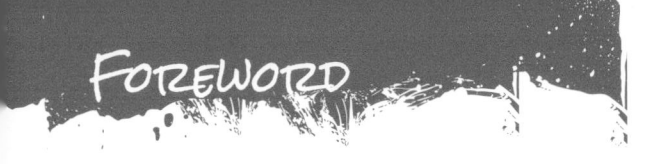

I'm so excited that you've decided to pick up this book! I can't tell you how much something like this would have meant to me when I was in high school in the early 2000s. Thinking back on that time, I can honestly say I don't recall ever reading anything positive about the LGBTQ community. And while *Will & Grace* was one of the most popular shows on television at the time, it never made me feel as though such stories could be a reality for me. That's in part why it took me nearly a decade more to finally come out in 2012 when I was 25 years old; I guess I knew so little about what it meant to be LGBTQ that I was never really able to come to terms with the fact that I was queer myself.

But times have changed so much since then. In the United States alone, marriage equality is now the law of the land; conversion therapy has been banned in more than 15 states (and counting!); all 50 states have been served by an openly LGBTQ-elected politician in some capacity at some time; and more LGBTQ artists and stories are being celebrated in music, film, and on television than ever before. And that's just the beginning! It's simply undeniable: *it gets better.*

After coming out and becoming the proud queer person I am today, I've made it my life's goal to help share information that lets others know that they're never alone. That's why I now work for the It Gets Better Project (www.itgetsbetter.org), a nonprofit with a mission to uplift, empower, and connect LGBTQ youth around the globe. The organization was founded in September 2010 when the first It Gets Better video was uploaded to YouTube. The viral online storytelling movement that quickly followed has generated over 60,000 video stories to date, one of the largest collections of LGBTQ stories the world has ever seen.

Since then, the It Gets Better Project has expanded into a global organization, working to tell stories and build communities everywhere. It does this through three core programs:

- **Media.** We continue to expand our story collection to reflect the vast diversity of the global LGBTQ community and to make it ever more accessible to LGBTQ youth everywhere. (See, itgetsbetter.org/stories.)
- **Global.** Through a growing network of affiliates, the It Gets Better Project is helping to equip communities with the knowledge, skills, and resources they need to tell their own stories. (See, itgetsbetter.org/global.)
- **Education.** It Gets Better stories have the power to inform our communities and inspire LGBTQ allies, which is why we're working to share them in as many classrooms and community spaces we can. (See, itgetsbetter.org/education.)

You can help the It Gets Better Project make a difference in the lives of LGBTQ young people everywhere. To get started, go to www.itgetsbetter.org and click "Get Involved." You can also help by sharing this book and the other incredible volumes from the LGBTQ Life series with someone you know and care about. You can also share them with a teacher or community leader, who will in turn share them with countless others. That's how movements get started.

In short, I'm so proud to play a role in helping to bring such an important collection like this to someone like you. I hope you enjoy each and every book, and please don't forget: *it gets better.*

Justin Tindall
Director, Education and
Global Programming
It Gets Better Project

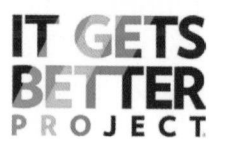

Introduction

Being LGBTQ is a great thing. But it's no secret that LGBTQ people face unique problems, especially young people. It's well known that school-age kids can be bullied for being different, and sometimes that can make them feel alone and excluded. It can affect how they see themselves and cause them to have low self-esteem, even depression. It's because of issues like this that the LGBTQ community has become such a strong and powerful place. LGBTQ people have learned how to have each other's backs. They've learned how to pick each other up when others are trying to tear them down. They've learned how to make each other feel supported and cared about. That's the power of community.

Like most words, *community* can be used in many different ways. Of course, a community can be a town, neighborhood, or city—when people form a community simply because they're in the same place. We also often use it just to mean *any* group of people. But the word has a deeper meaning when we talk about communities like the LGBTQ community. Fabian Pfortmuller, who helps people build communities professionally, wrote on the Web site Medium his definition of this type of community: "a group of people that care about each other and feel they belong together."

He explains the "care about each other" portion of that definition: "The individuals in a group are not just random strangers, they have relationships with each other. . . . They care more about the people in this group than about the average person they meet on the street. This is where the magic of a community happens. When people care about each other, they develop trust. And trust unlocks collaboration, sharing, support, hope, safety and much more."

It's common for LGBTQ people to feel a connection with others based on that shared characteristic of sexual orientation or gender orientation. There's something about having something that important in common with each other that links people, even people who have no other connection.

Further, he explains the other part of the definition, "feel they belong together": "Communities address one of the most fundamental human needs: we want to be loved, we don't want to be lonely and we want to know that we belong somewhere. Real communities give us this sense of home, this sense of family, this sense of 'these are my peers.' This is my tribe, this is where I belong. In this group, I am being accepted for who I really am."

In other words, community is whoever makes us feel understood, accepted, and supported. Unsurprisingly, psychologists have found that those with strong community support are less likely to experience depression and are better able to handle difficult circumstances that might come up in life. Community makes us stronger.

Community is not a passive thing. It is something that we actively participate in, whether we realize that is what's happening or not. When your friend is having a bad day, and you tell them you know how they feel, you are helping them feel understood. When your parent helps you finish your homework, they are showing that they support you. And when someone lets you know that they understand what you are going through and that they accept you and love you as an LGBTQ person, they are showing you that you are part of their community.

This is what the LGBTQ community is for many people. When so much of the world has not been accepting, LGBTQ people have looked to each other for support and acceptance.

The purpose of this book is either to help you find that community while still in school, or if you're not able or ready to do that right now, to help you see the community that will be there waiting for you when you are ready.

Chapter 1 introduces you to the idea of what it means to be LGBTQ. Chapter 2 shows you opportunities for community that may be available to you in your local area. Chapter 3 gives information about how to find community online. Chapter 4 shows you the diversity within the LGBTQ community and how that can help you find people who understand more than one aspect of who you are. Finally,

Chapter 5 breaks down how your community can change over time and in different contexts.

No matter your race, religion, or personal interests, there is a niche for you within the LGBTQ community and a support network of countless LGBTQ people who understand what you're going through and how you feel. It's possible to find a place where you fit. It's possible to find people who understand you and support you. It may take some work and some patience, but it's worth it.

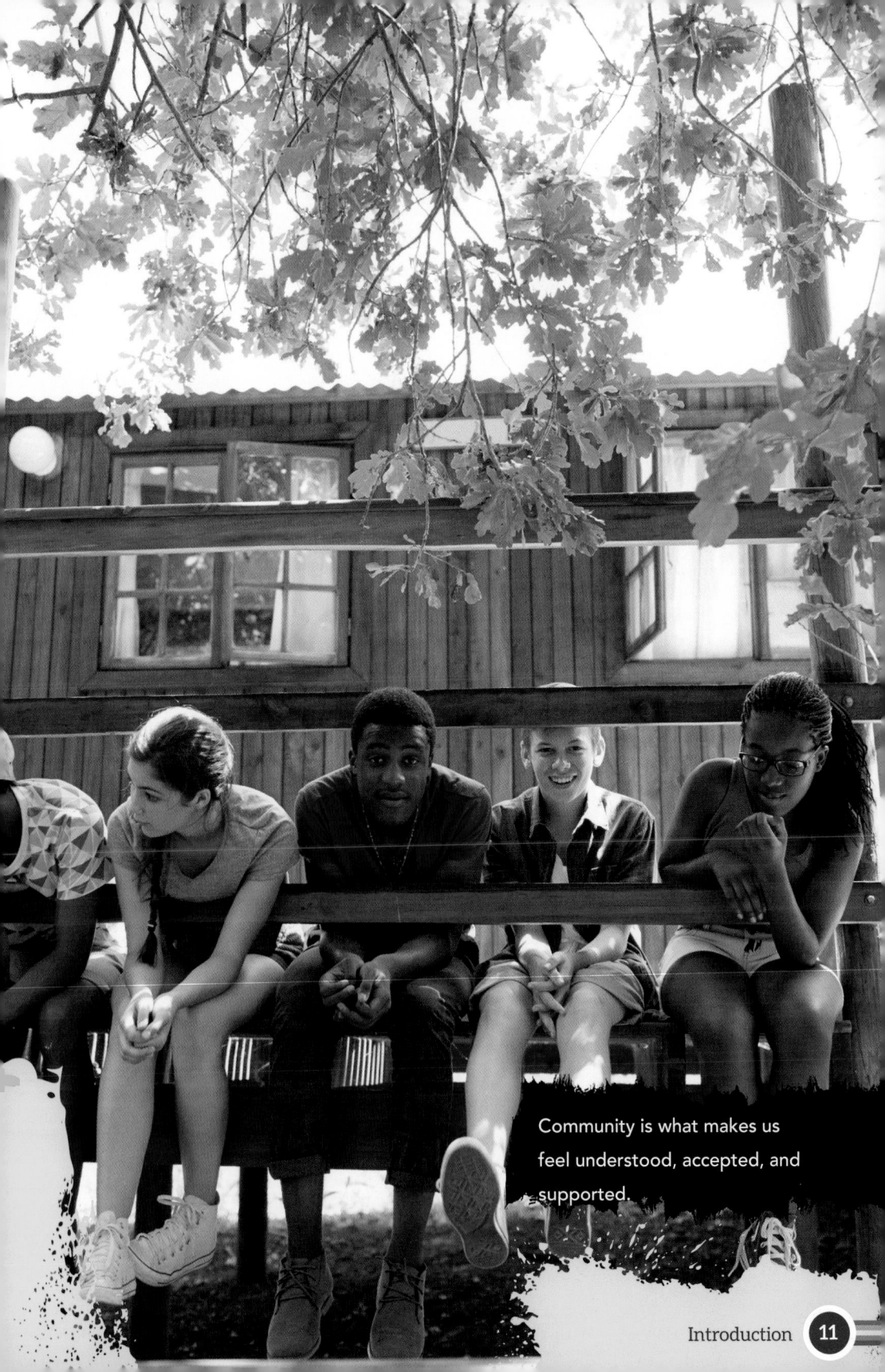

Community is what makes us feel understood, accepted, and supported.

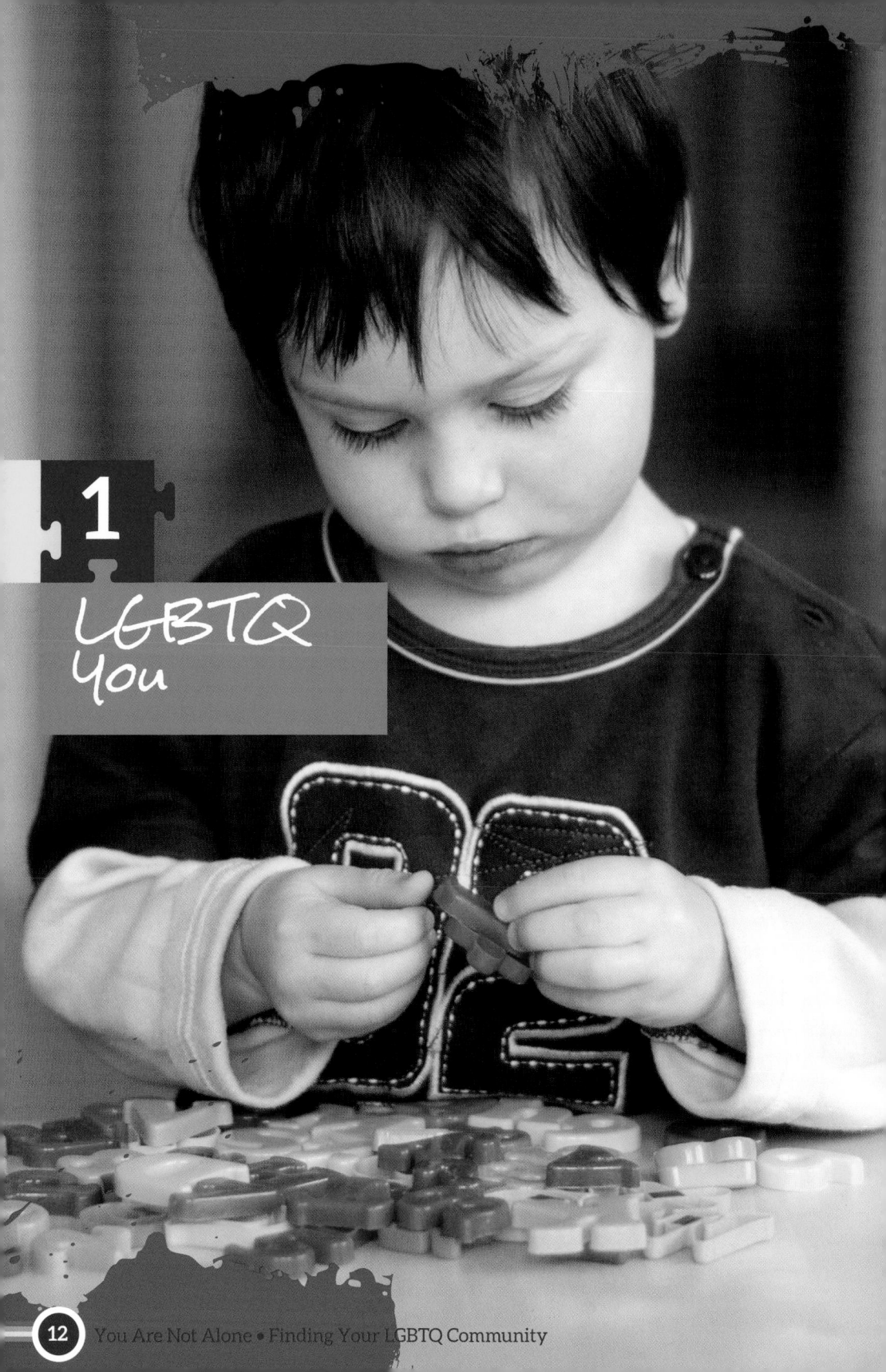

1

LGBTQ You

WORDS TO UNDERSTAND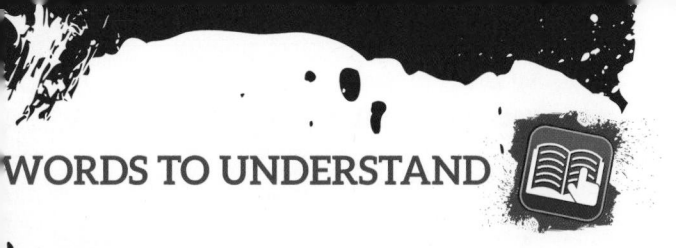

ASEXUAL: *A person who feels very little or no sexual attraction to people of any gender.*

GENDERQUEER: *When a person doesn't identify as only male or female. They could identity as neither gender or some combination of both.*

IDENTITY: *How people define themselves, including all aspects they consider important to who they are.*

PANSEXUAL: *A person whose attraction to a person is independent of that person's gender.*

STEREOTYPE: *Using one aspect of a person to make assumptions about the rest of who they are.*

Born as a biological girl, Jamie was always just thought of as a tomboy. But he felt there was more to it. "I had always just thought I was a boy when I was a really young kid, and then as I grew up I realized that I was different. I felt like I just needed to fit in and live as female. I felt very uncomfortable. I had these feelings, but I didn't know how to describe them. I didn't know what I was feeling was possible and was a real thing that I could do something about."

It wasn't until later that he found the word to put to what he was experiencing. "The light bulb moment came when I was sixteen, and I just happened to watch a documentary about a young trans guy," he said on his YouTube channel, Jammidodger. "I made this huge discovery about myself, and I finally had a way to describe how I was feeling." Watching the documentary and realizing there were others like him also allowed Jamie to "accept it about myself." Realizing his **identity** as a transgender man also gave him the ability to find others like him who could relate to what he was going through.

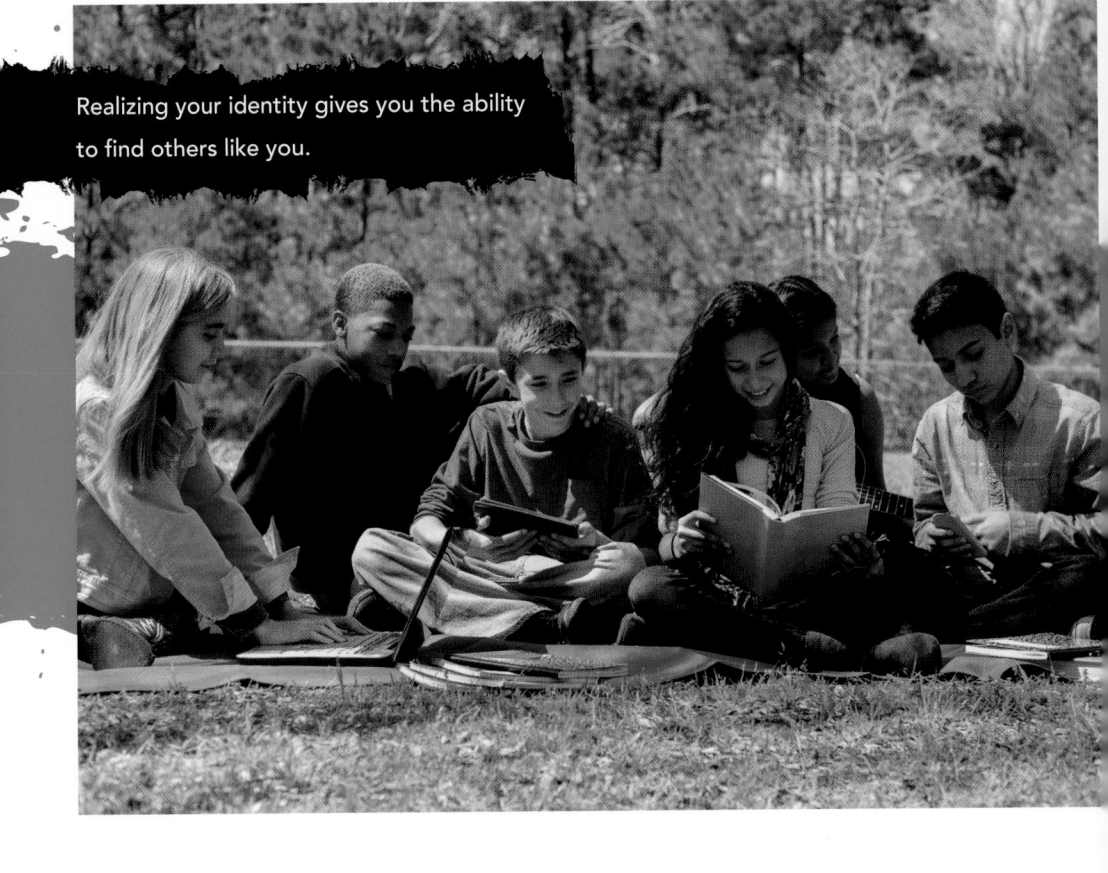

Realizing your identity gives you the ability to find others like you.

Though Jamie's experience was figuring out that he was transgender, many other types of LGBTQ people have similar experiences figuring out their identity over time.

WHAT AN IDENTITY MEANS ... AND WHAT IT DOESN'T MEAN

Every person is more than just one thing. A person is not *only* LGBTQ. They are also right- or left-handed. They are blond-, brown-, black-, or red-haired. They are Latino, African American, Asian, Native American, white, mixed race, or another race. They have different interests, strengths, and weaknesses. And there are so many other aspects of you that make you who you are. These are all parts of your identity. When you "identify as" something, it means you are saying that thing is a part of your identity.

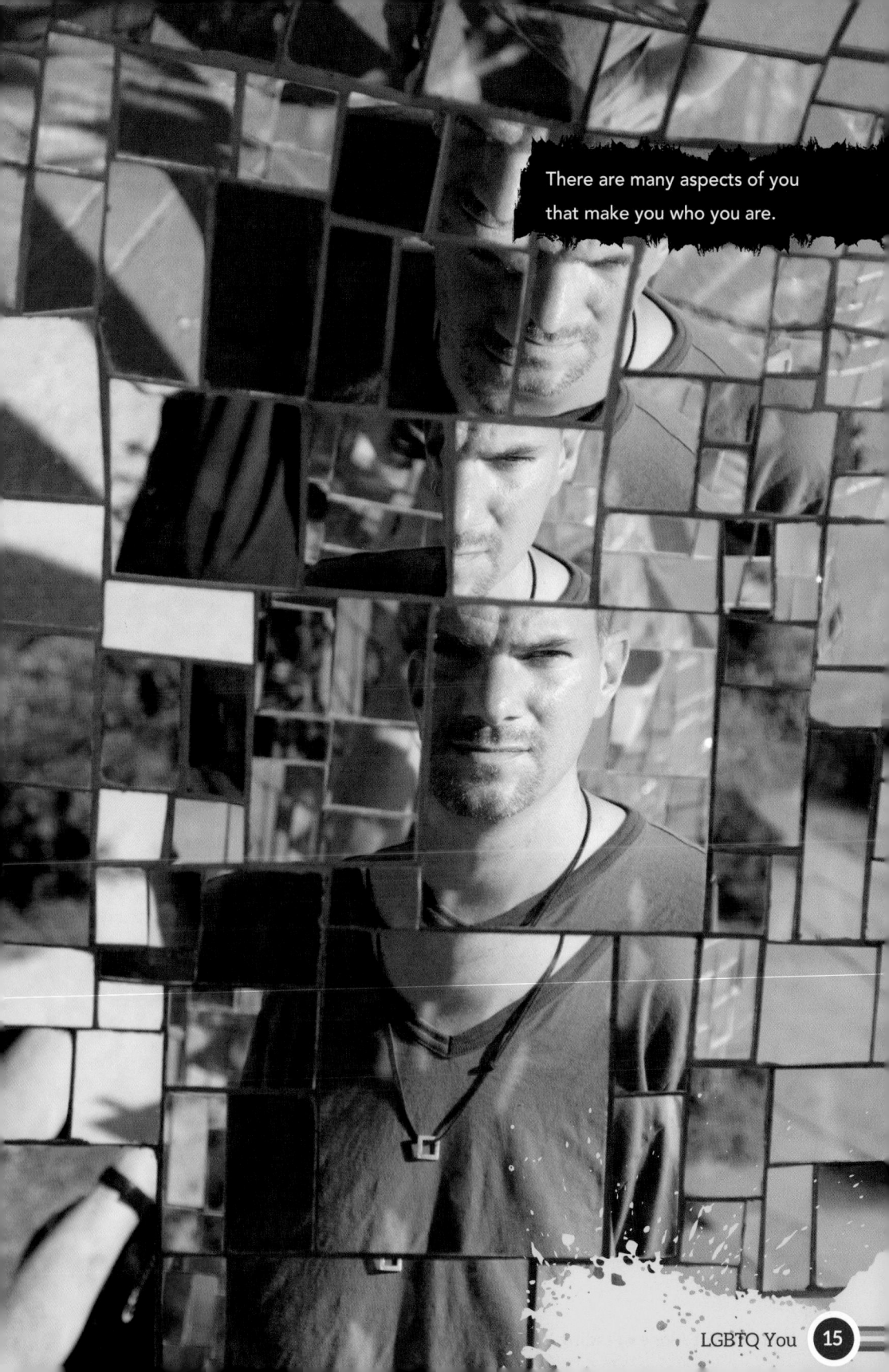

There are many aspects of you
that make you who you are.

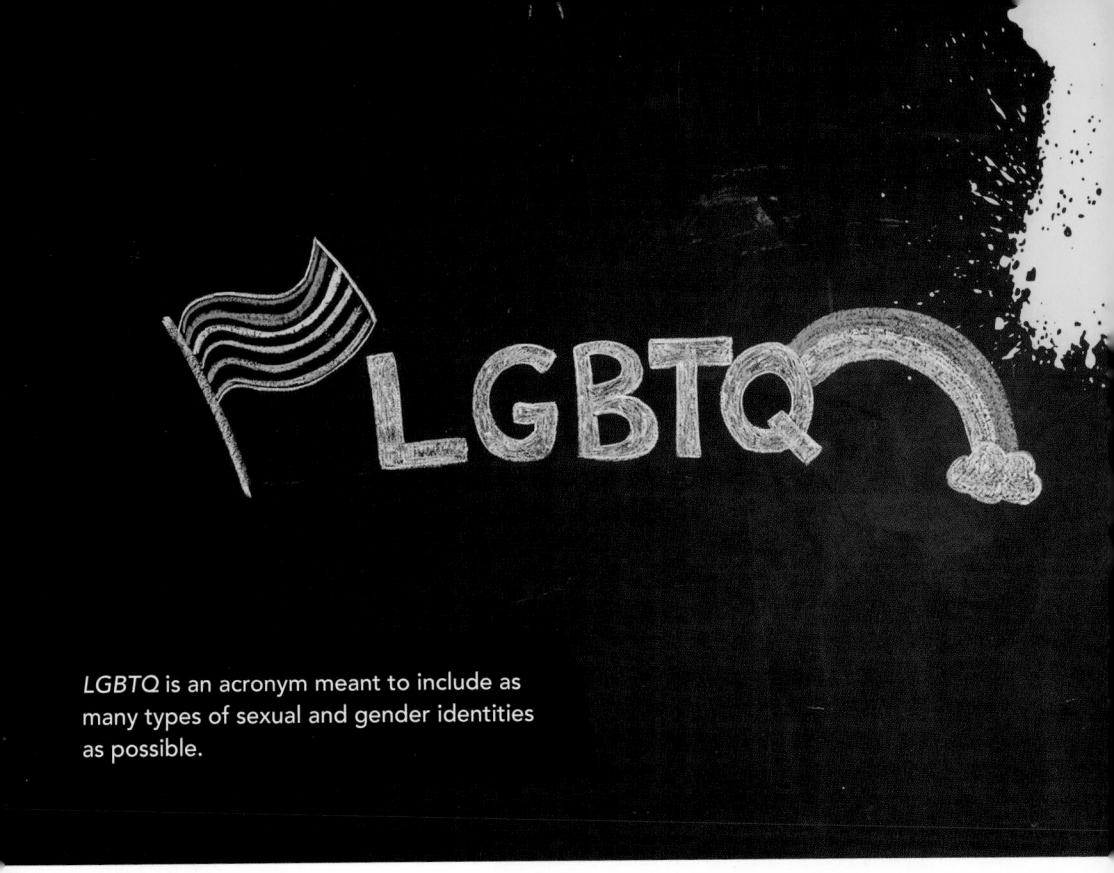

LGBTQ is an acronym meant to include as many types of sexual and gender identities as possible.

LGBTQ is an acronym meant to include as many types of sexual and gender identities as possible. The L stands for *lesbian*, or women who are attracted to women. The G stands for *gay*, meaning men who are attracted to men (though *gay* is also sometimes used to refer to lesbians or even all sexual minorities). The B stands for *bisexual*, meaning men or women who are attracted to both men and women. The T in LGBTQ stands for *transgender*, meaning persons who identify with a different gender from the one they were assigned at birth. A person might seem like a male to other people but identify as a woman, or look like a female to other people but identify as a man. The Q in LGBTQ can mean *questioning*, meaning persons who are still figuring out how they identify. The Q can also stand for *queer*.

The word *queer* is complicated. It can be used in many different ways. For a long time, it was used as an insult, and for some people

it still feels that way. Within the LGBTQ movement, queer is often used to refer to all sexual minorities. Queer is also sometimes used to refer to people who are sexual minorities but don't fit within the *L, G, B,* or *T.* This can include people who are **genderqueer**, which means that they don't identify with either gender or purposely try to blur the lines between what is considered male and female. It can also include people who are **asexual**, meaning they feel no or very little sexual attraction to anyone. A **pansexual** person is someone who would say that their attraction to a person has nothing to do with the gender of that person. All of these identities—and more—can be considered part of the *Q* in *LGBTQ.*

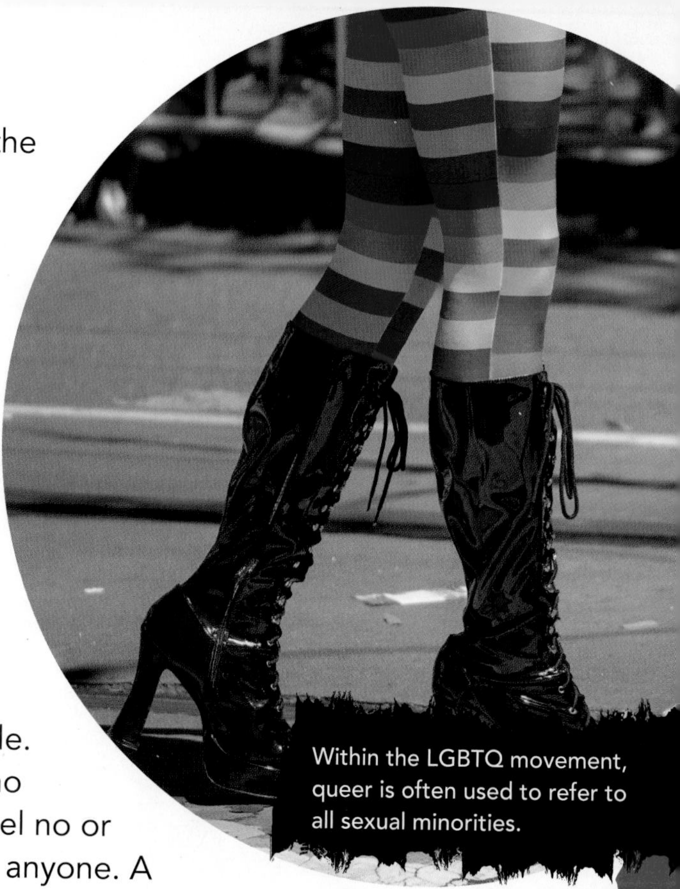

Within the LGBTQ movement, queer is often used to refer to all sexual minorities.

It's important to note the difference between sexual identity and gender identity. *Sexual identity* refers to people to whom you are romantically or sexually attracted. *Gender identity* means which gender or lack of gender you feel most represents who you are. These two things aren't necessarily tied together. For example, a transgender man is not always attracted to women.

LGBTQ 101
An Introduction to the Queer Community

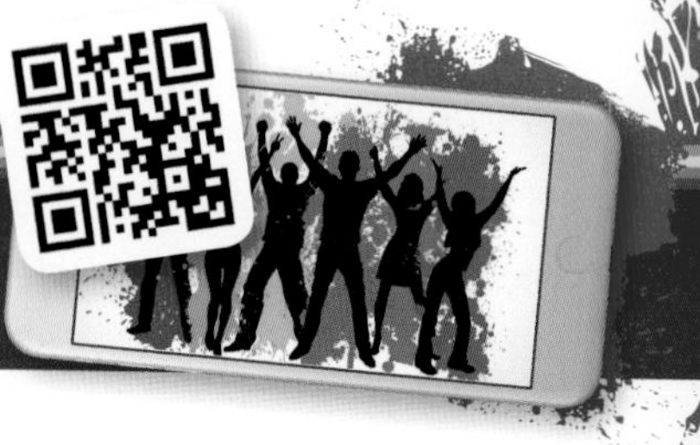

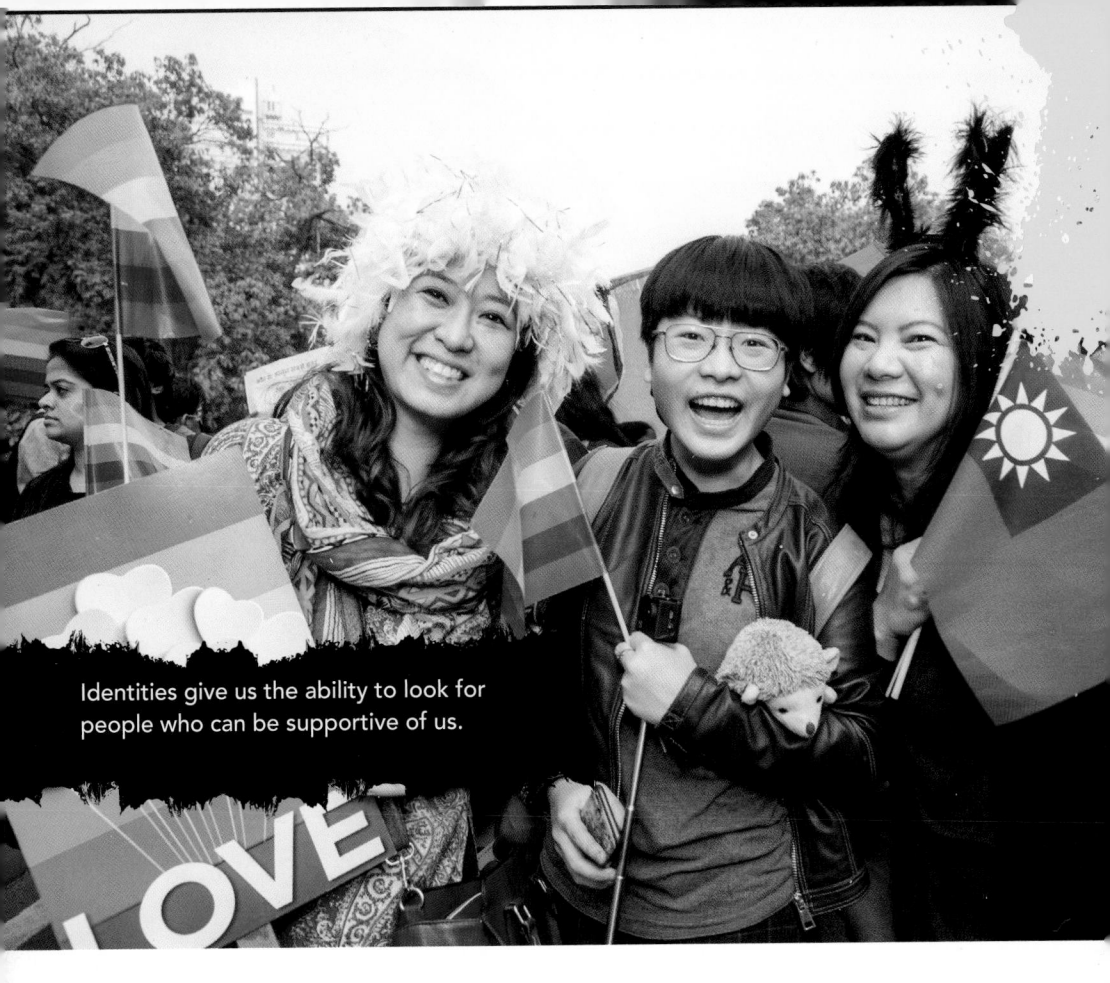

Identities give us the ability to look for people who can be supportive of us.

HOW LABELS CAN HELP AND HURT

Labelling our identities can be helpful in some ways. They can help us explain ourselves to others. If we come out to someone as LGBTQ, that gives them some idea of what we're going through. The labels can help to communicate to others fundamental truths about ourselves. Identities can help us find community. They give us the ability to look for others like ourselves and for people who can be supportive of us.

Labels can be a problem sometimes, too, though. They are an attempt to make something very complex seem simple. A person's sexuality or gender identity is difficult to reduce to a one-word

description. Sometimes these words fall short of adequately describing people's identities, so don't panic if none of these words seems to describe you perfectly.

Another way that labels can cause problems is that people will often try to reduce a person to just that one characteristic. They think that if they know one thing about a person, they know everything about that person. They think that they can predict how a

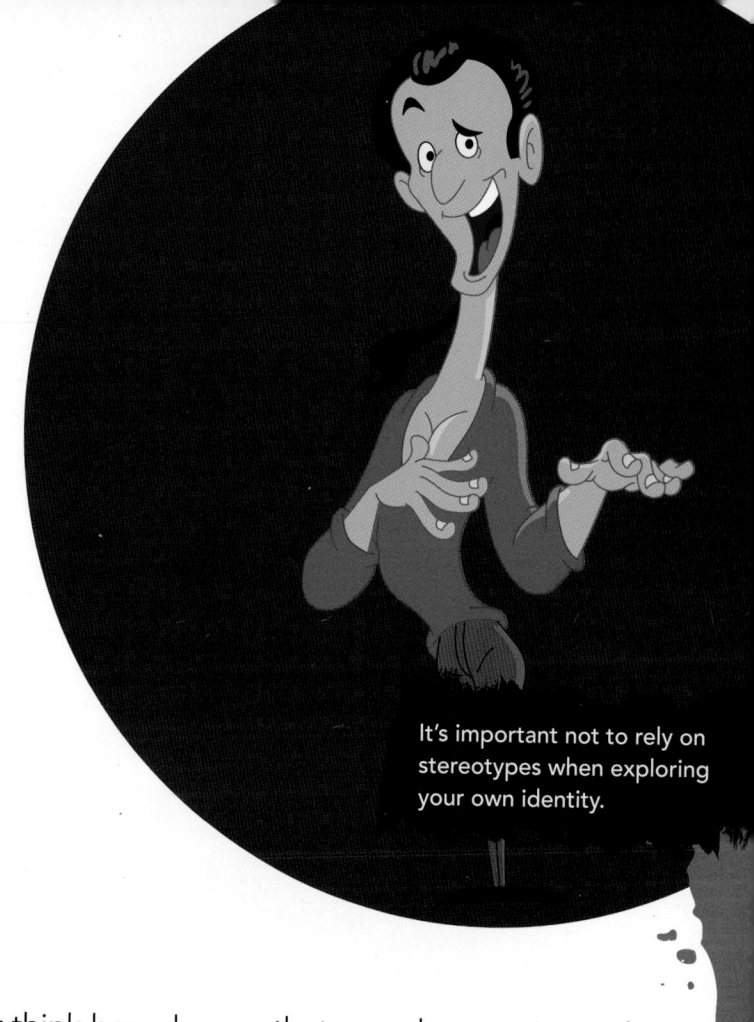

It's important not to rely on stereotypes when exploring your own identity.

person is going to act or think based upon that one characteristic. This is called a **stereotype**.

Some of the assumptions are somewhat harmless and just come from misinformed people who don't know what being LGBTQ really means. But some stereotypes can be very harmful, making people assume that all LGBTQ people have certain negative traits.

Stereotypes can affect a person's self-image, too. The way others see us can affect how we see ourselves. If society has taught us our entire lives that LGBTQ people act a certain way, we may assume that they are right, and we may feel that we have to be that way or risk not being accepted. It's important to not rely upon these stereotypes when exploring your own identity.

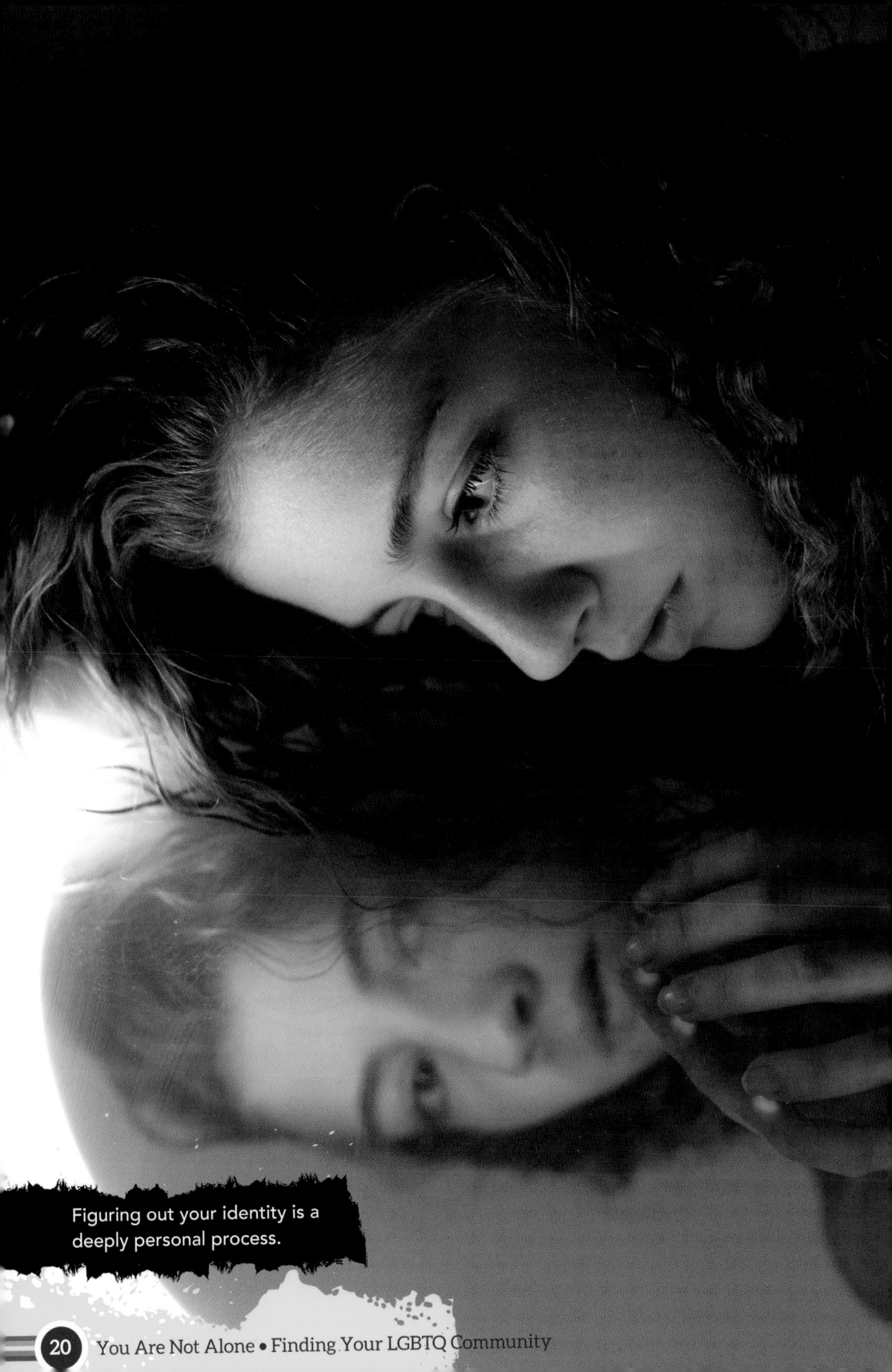

Figuring out your identity is a deeply personal process.

WHAT IS MY SEXUAL IDENTITY?

Figuring out your identity is a deeply personal process. There is no wrong or right way to do so. It can be hard to know where to begin, though. The Web site Teen Health Source (teenhealthsource.com) gives some advice on questions to ask yourself to begin to figure out what your sexual identity is:

"What attracts me to different people?"

"What and who are my sexual fantasies focused on?"

"What types of bodies, acts, and porn/erotica arouse me, and why?"

"If I had a sexual encounter with a member of the same sex, do I think I would enjoy it and want to do it again?"

FINDING IDENTITY

Some people seem to know exactly who they are and what they stand for without struggling with it. But realizing your identity may take longer and require more thought and consideration. You may remember your first crush as a small child being someone of the same sex. You may remember realizing you were more comfortable in clothes associated with the opposite gender. You may remember when you first started noticing the bodies of people you weren't expected to notice. These are good ways of figuring out for yourself what your sexuality and gender identity are. For many people, this is how a realization of their identities begin.

For many people, though, forming identities and embracing them are more difficult processes. The sidebars in this chapter provide some advice on how to explore your identity if you're unsure.

Bella Qvist has found that her search for identity extends even past deciding whom she wants to be in a relationship with. "My girlfriend's been a lesbian for as long as she can remember, my good friend was always bi, and I have many friends who call themselves queer.

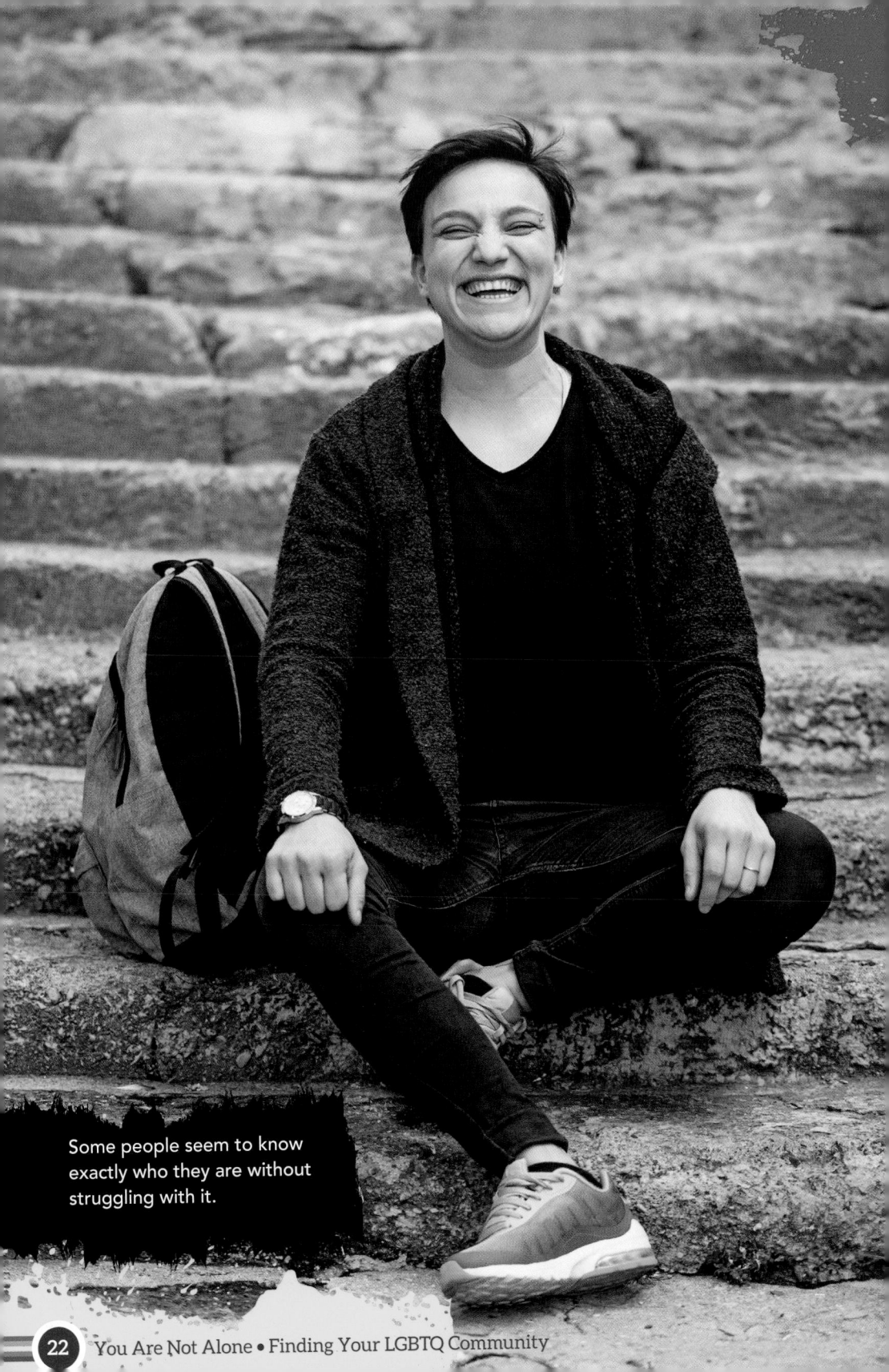

Some people seem to know exactly who they are without struggling with it.

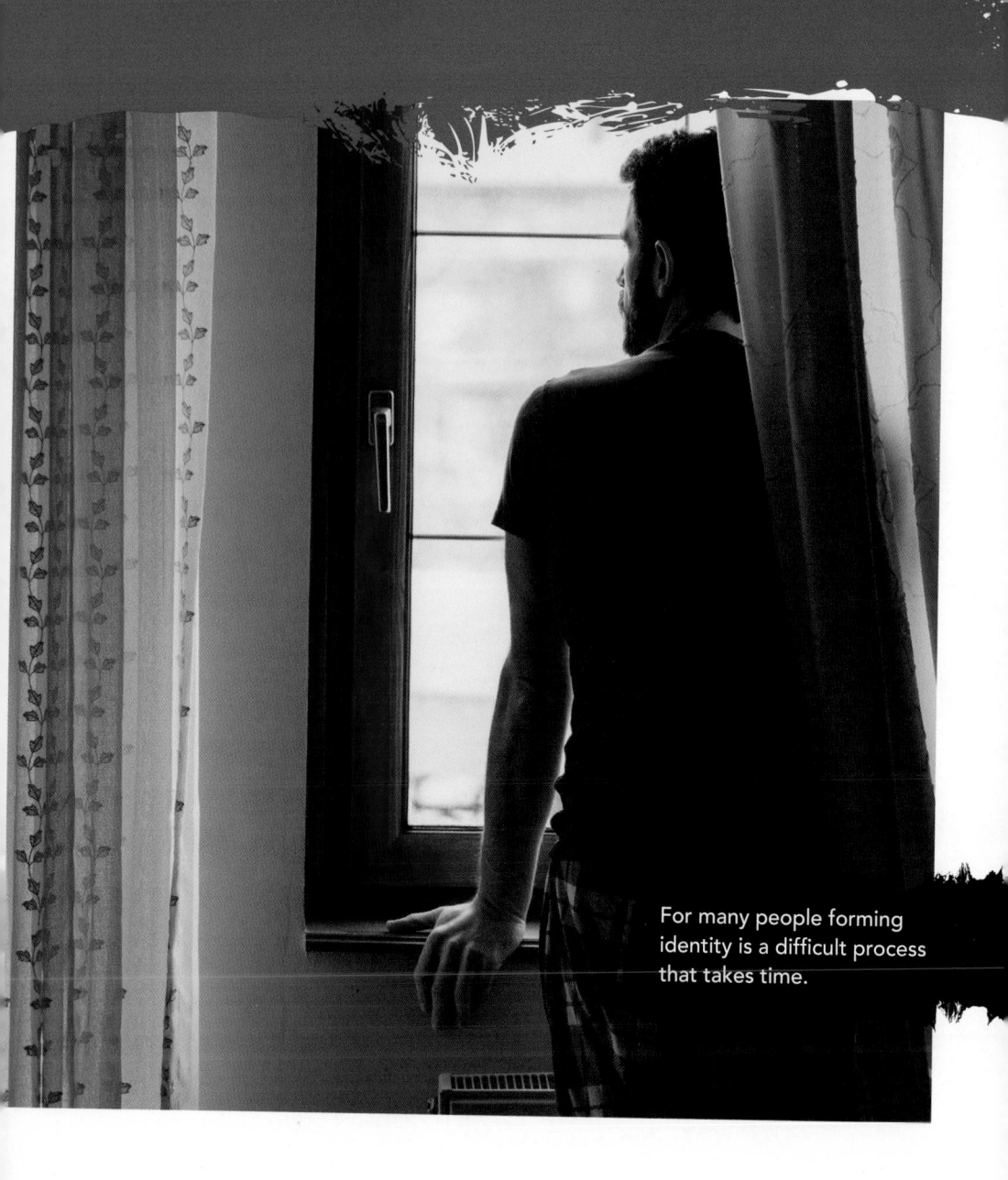

For many people forming identity is a difficult process that takes time.

But for me, approximately three years into a life of being out, these labels don't sit right. Do I have to settle with one?" she writes to the *Guardian* newspaper. The answer is no, you don't have to settle with one. The words we attach to identities are meant to help you and those you want to share them with to understand what is going on inside of you. If none of these words helps you to do that, you don't have to pick one.

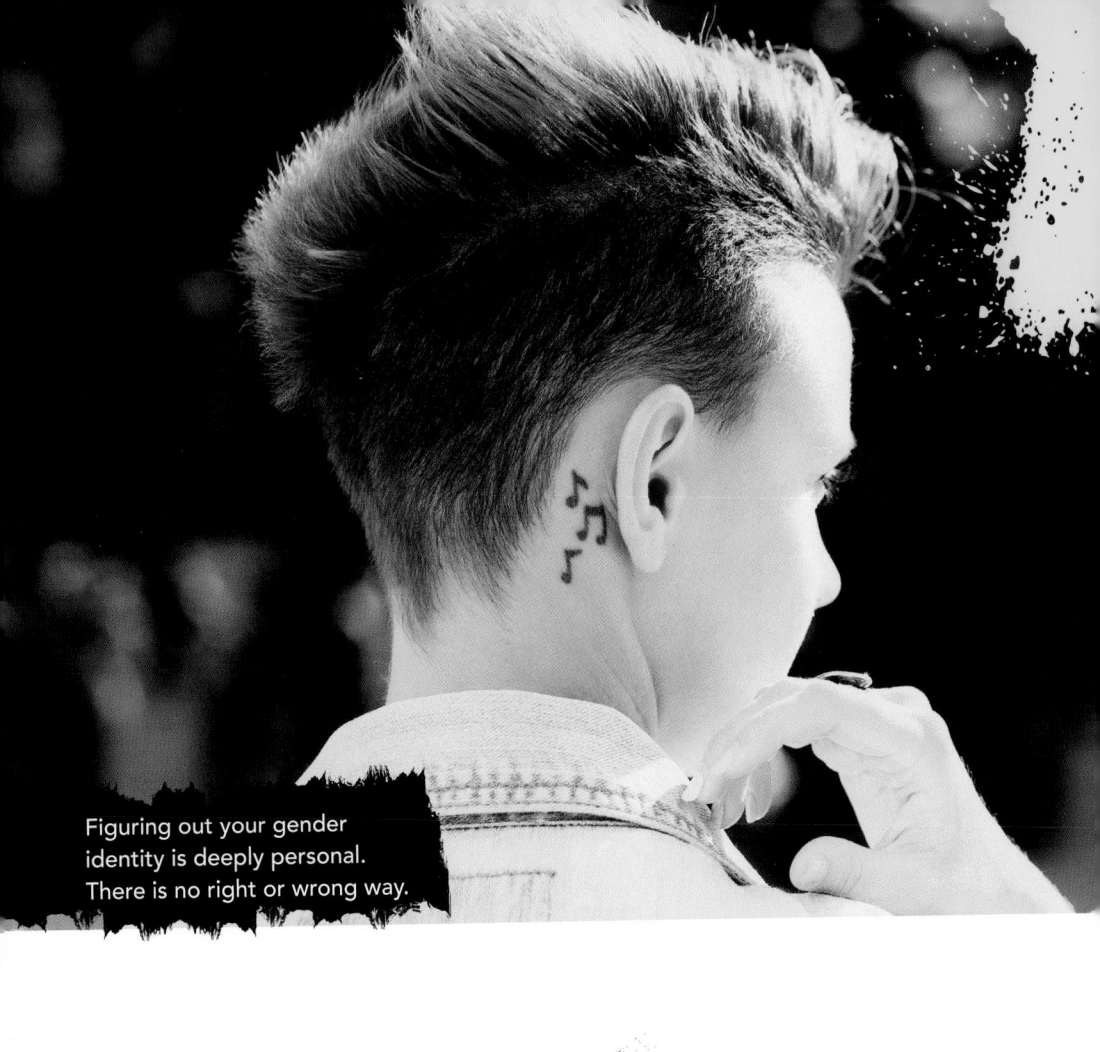

Figuring out your gender identity is deeply personal. There is no right or wrong way.

WHAT IS MY GENDER IDENTITY?

Similar to sexual identity, figuring out your gender identity is a deeply personal process. There is no wrong or right way to do so. It can be hard to know where to begin though. The Web site Teen Health Source (teenhealthsource.com) gives some advice on questions to ask yourself to begin to figure out what your gender identity is:

"What gender do I feel most comfortable expressing myself in?"

"Do I feel comfortable with my biological sex?"

"Am I comfortable or uncomfortable with my sex-specific body parts? (For example, do I have breasts and wish I didn't?)"

"Do I wish I had body parts I don't have?"

If you do pick one, remember that word does not define everything about you. As the LGBTQ rights organization Human Rights Campaign (HRC) point out on its Web site, sometimes people "feel pressure to prioritize their different identities." Instead of giving in to that pressure, "we must find a way to show our peers that you don't have to pick just one identity. . . . We have to be honest with ourselves and embrace all the parts of ourselves, because that's when we're at our strongest."

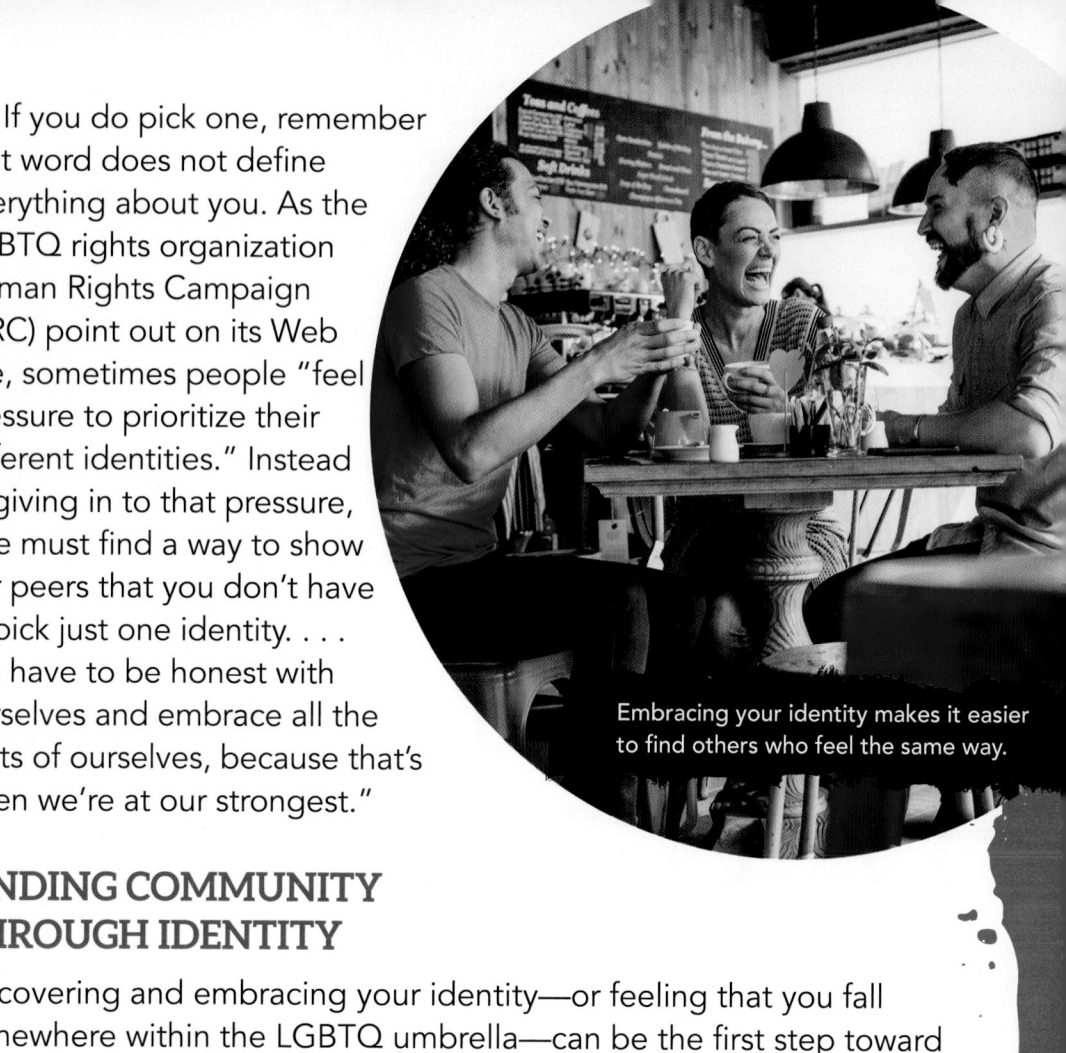

Embracing your identity makes it easier to find others who feel the same way.

FINDING COMMUNITY THROUGH IDENTITY

Discovering and embracing your identity—or feeling that you fall somewhere within the LGBTQ umbrella—can be the first step toward finding a community that can understand and support you in your sexual and gender identity. It makes it easier to find others who feel the same way.

When you go to find community, you take with you everything that you are, not just your identity as an LGBTQ person. We are all complex, multi-faceted people who should be respected and loved for all parts of ourselves. That's true of you, and it's also true of the people you will be meeting. Just as you don't want others to make assumptions about you, you should avoid making assumptions about what you will find when you go out to find community. You may be surprised at the types of people you will meet. As you approach finding your LGBTQ community, keep an open mind.

We all should be respected and loved for all parts of ourselves.

TEXT-DEPENDENT QUESTIONS

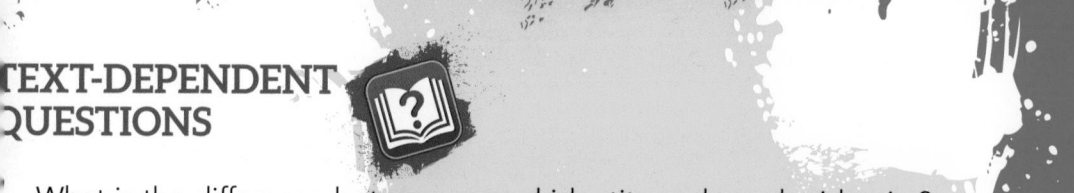

1. What is the difference between sexual identity and gender identity?

2. What do the letters in *LGBTQ* stand for?

3. What are some of the meanings of the word *queer*?

RESEARCH PROJECTS

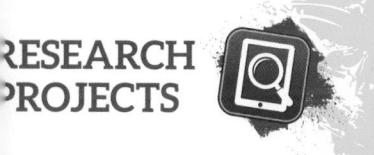

1. Take some time to think about your own identity. Ask yourself the questions from Teen Health Source listed above. You may find it helpful to write out your answers. Remember, you don't have to have a final answer right now! Just take some time to honestly analyze how you feel.

2. Watch the Queer Community video (www.youtube.com/watch?v= DE7bKmOXY3w), and make a list of the names of some of the other types of identities that are possible. In your own words, write out what these labels mean.

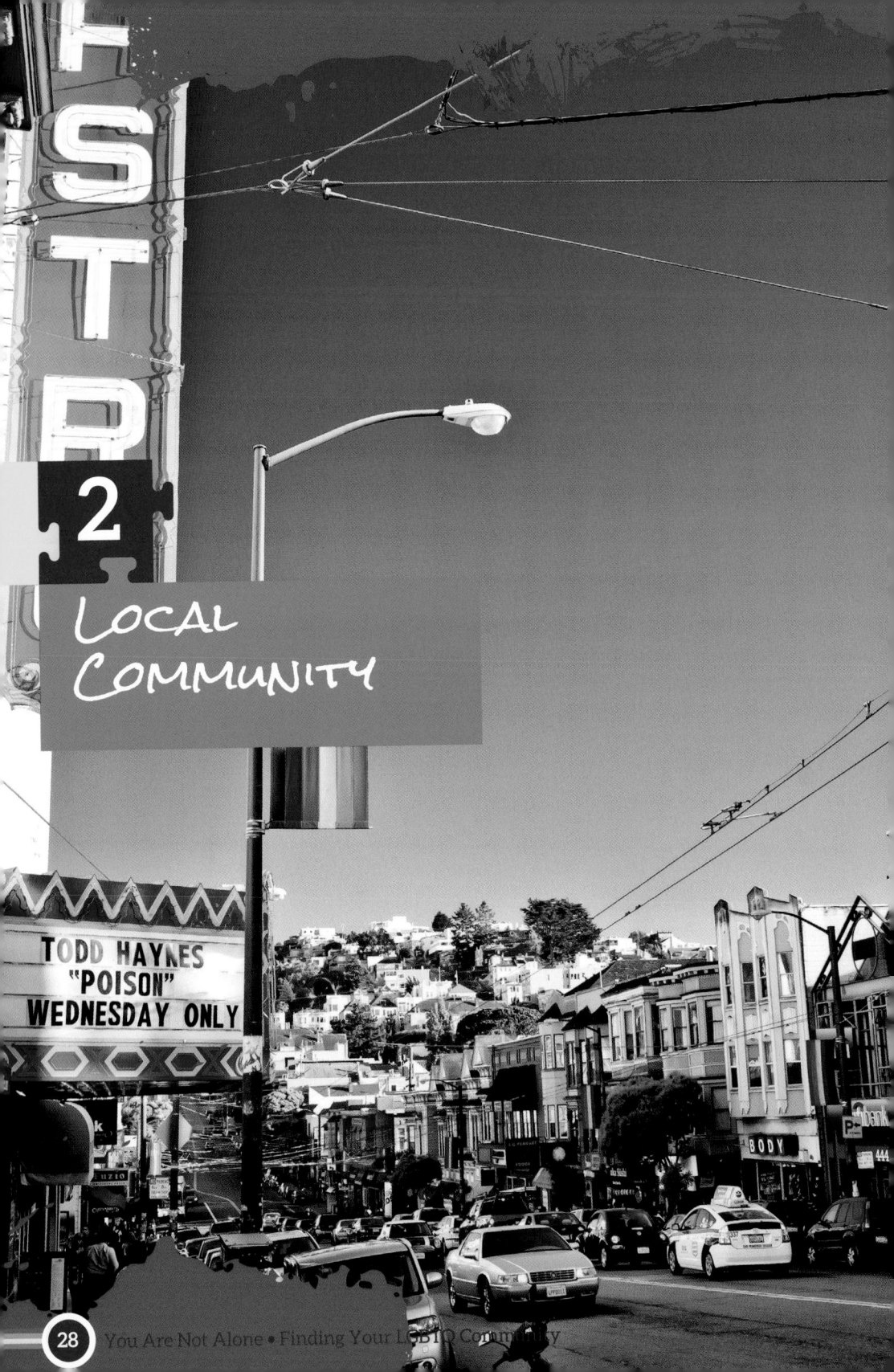

2

LOCAL
COMMUNITY

WORDS TO UNDERSTAND

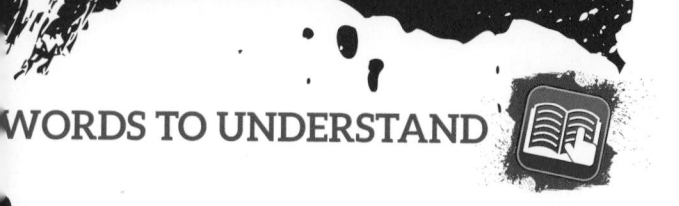

ALLIES: *Non-LGBTQ people who are supportive of LGBTQ people and their cause.*

GAYBORHOOD: *A gay neighborhood. The part of a city where LGBTQ businesses and organizations are likely to be found.*

INCLUSIVE: *Allowing everyone to be a part of something, regardless of who or what they are.*

In the past, before the Internet and before sexual and gender minorities began to be more accepted, LGBTQ people's greatest hope for finding **inclusive** community was to move to a city that was known to have a large number of others like them. Places like San Francisco and New York City became centers of the LGBTQ community that drew people from all over the country, even the world.

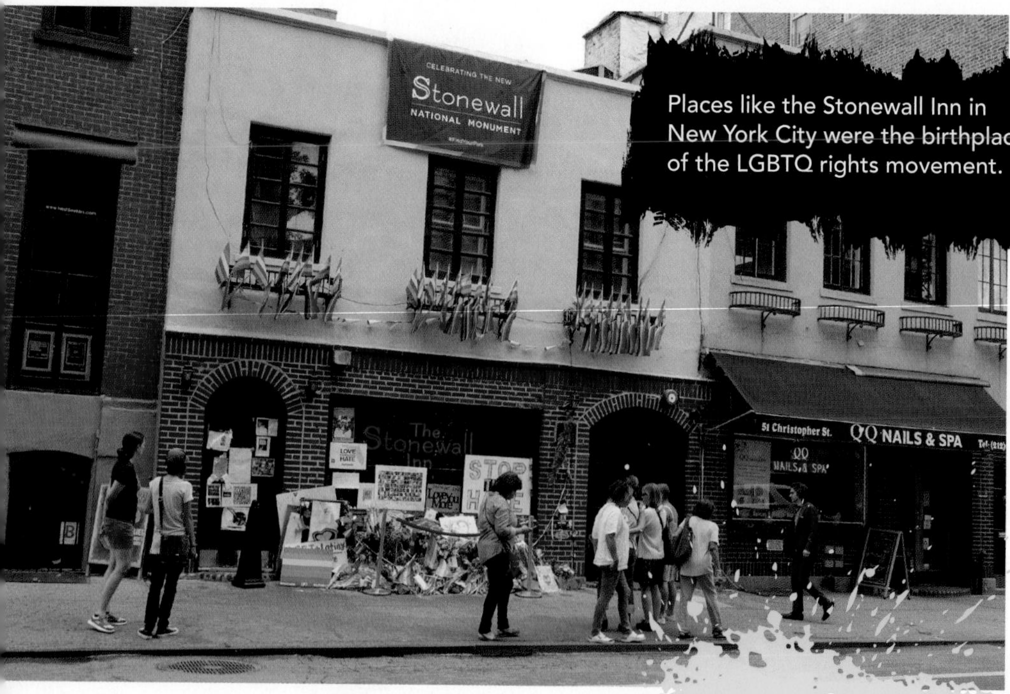

Places like the Stonewall Inn in New York City were the birthplaces of the LGBTQ rights movement.

It was these local communities that produced a lot of the things that we consider part of the LGBTQ culture, like Pride parades, gay bars, and community centers. These places were also the birthplaces of the LGBTQ rights movement. Though our options for community now are more diverse, local community continues to be an important element of the LGBTQ life.

Fortunately, it's often no longer necessary to move somewhere just to find a community. It's especially fortunate, since young people aren't able to choose to do that on their own! It's now possible to find local community in many cities and towns of all sizes.

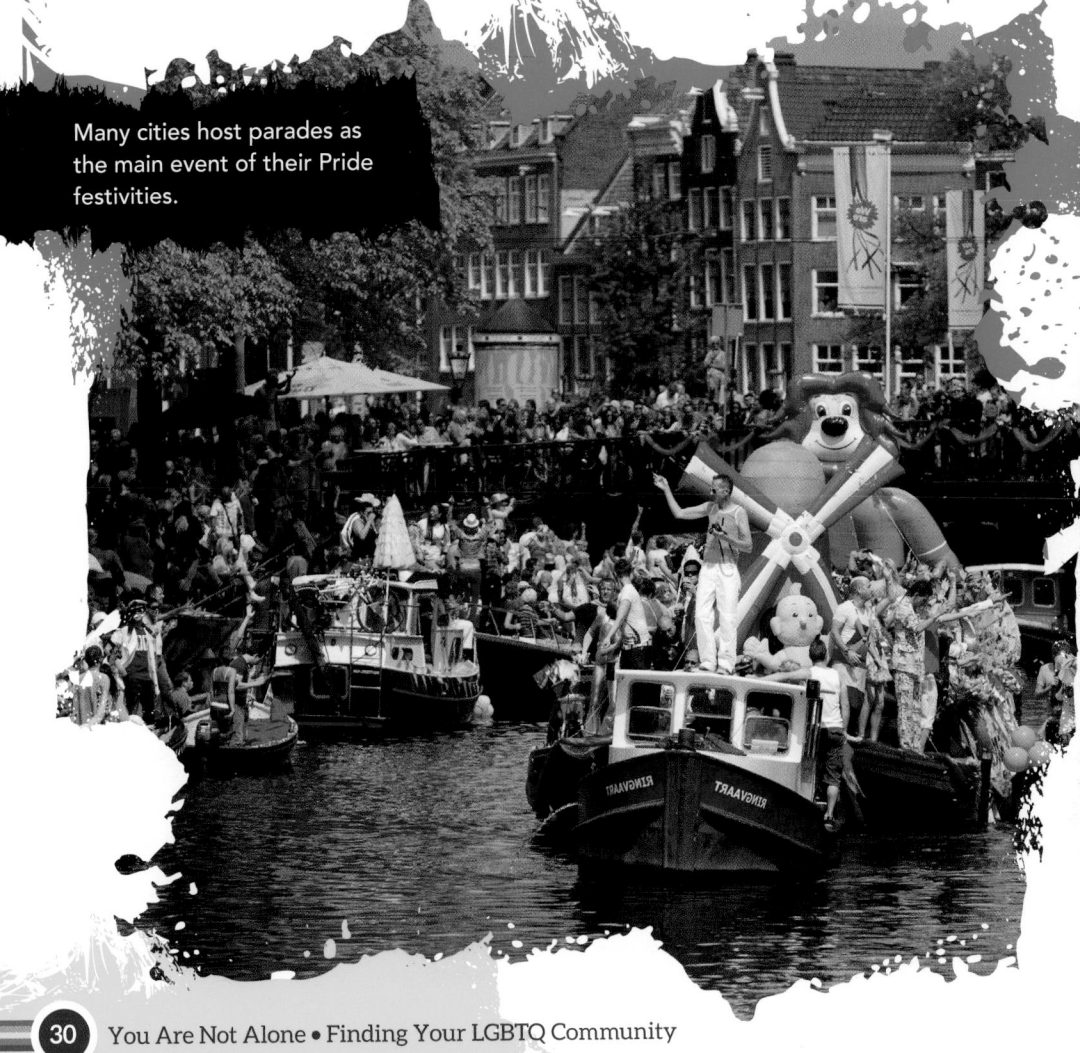

Many cities host parades as the main event of their Pride festivities.

PRIDE

Often, the most visible signs of an LGBTQ community are Pride parades and festivals. These are events that are held in many cities around the world where people come together to show solidarity and to be around others like them. Different cities have different types of events that are included in their Pride festivities. Many have parades that people march in. Sometimes these parades have more of a protest-like feel to them, with signs and banners that advocate for LGBTQ rights. Others have more of a feeling of celebration, with groups of people representing various organizations gathering to show solidarity with, and support for, the LGBTQ community.

The parades will often end at the location of the Pride festivals, where booths are set up for organizations that offer various services to the LGBTQ community. Businesses and other groups who are supportive are also represented with booths. Pride parades and festivals can be a great introduction to the gay community. Being in such a large crowd of like-minded people can bring an incredible feeling of unity.

LGBTQ AT SCHOOL

Adolescence is hard for most people, but for LGBTQ kids, it can be especially hard. A lot of society still isn't accepting of LGBTQ people, and the kids at school can reflect that. Bullying is still a major issue for a lot of people. Finding a supportive community at school can be a huge help in navigating these difficult years.

Many schools now have groups called GSAs, or Genders and Sexualities Alliances, though they are sometimes referred to by their old name, Gay–Straight Alliances. These are clubs that serve as inclusive safe zones for people of all sexualities and gender identities. According the GSA Network Web site (gsanetwork.org), "Every GSA can create its own mission and goals to meet the different needs of its members and their individual school climates."

GSAs can fall under three categories or some combination of the three, according to GSA Network. "Social GSAs'" primary purpose

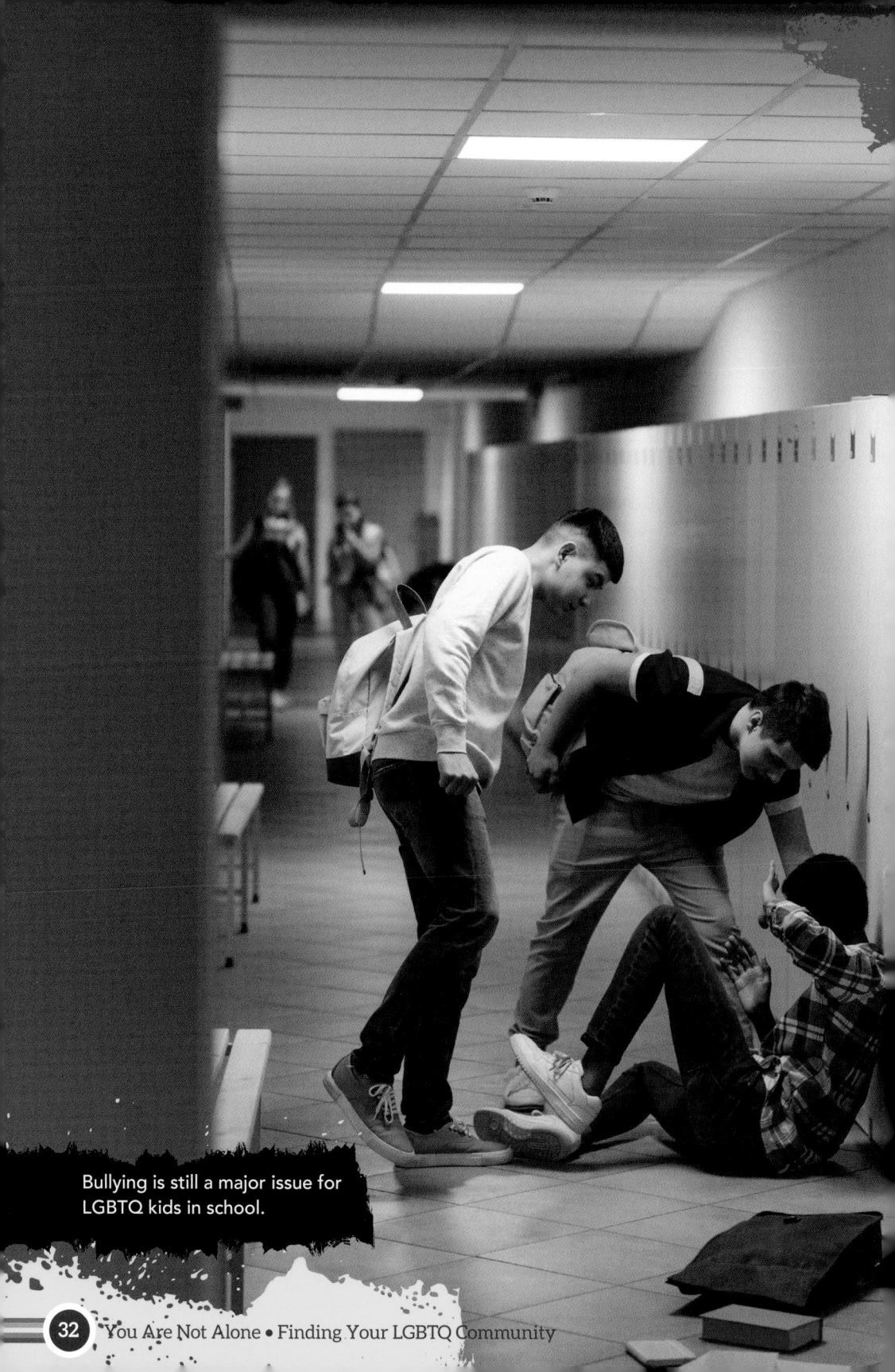

Bullying is still a major issue for LGBTQ kids in school.

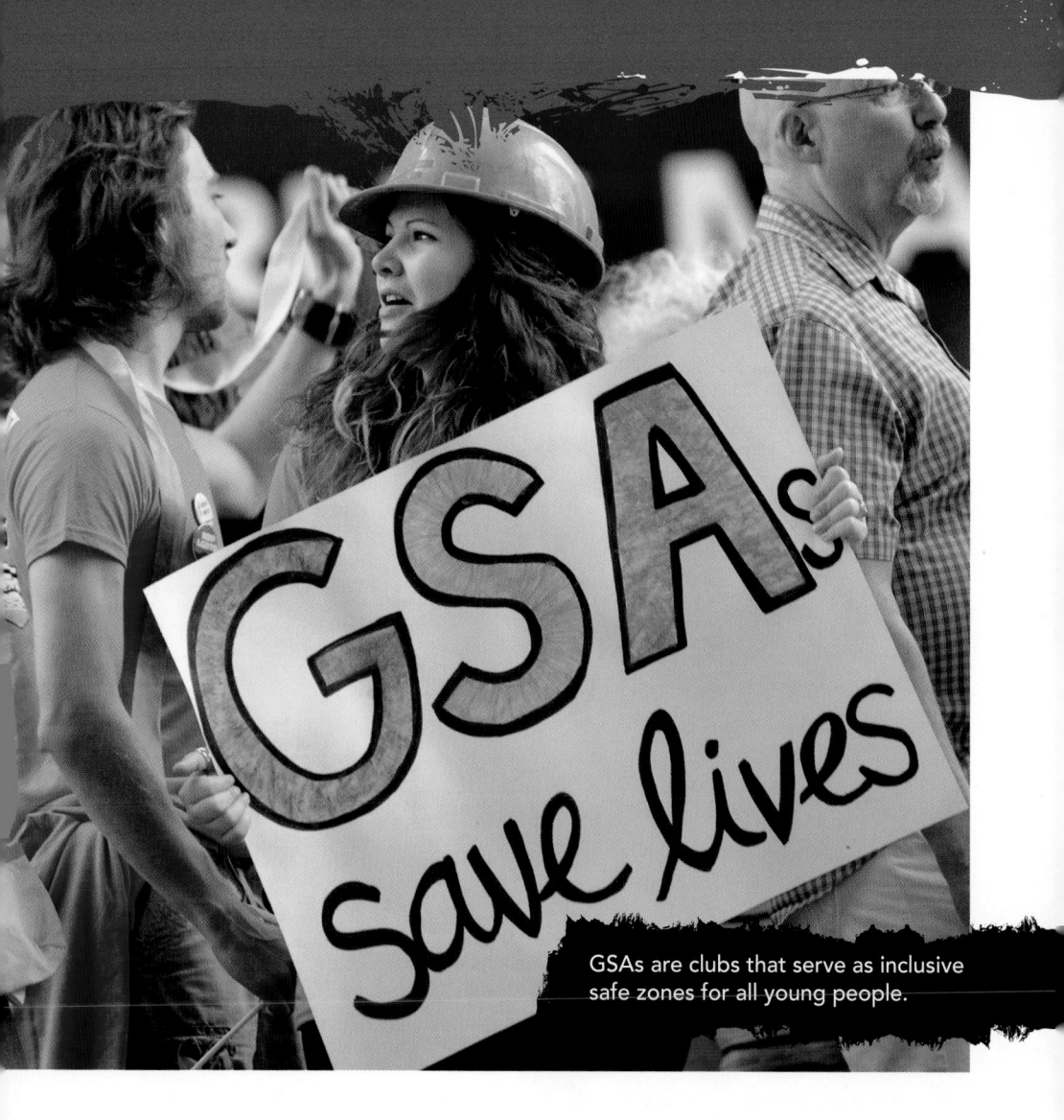

GSAs are clubs that serve as inclusive safe zones for all young people.

to help "students meet and connect with other trans and queer tudents on campus." "Support GSAs" are meant to "work to create afe spaces and talk about the various issues they face in school or heir broader community, such as discrimination from teachers or chool administrators." "Activist GSAs" are for students who want to take a leadership role to improve school climate through campaigns nd events that raise awareness and change policies or practices in heir schools."

Diana Tourjée's school's GSA made a big difference in her life. It was a small club, she wrote on the Web site Broadly. "In fact, there weren't many members at all, but we did our best to support each other, and the GSA was a valuable lifeline at a time in my life when I felt alienated and lost. We talked about some of the difficult things we were going through … and we talked about other things, things that made us happy. We learned about LGBTQ movies and books, slowly mapping out the American LGBTQ community's piecemeal history of beauty, survival, oppression, resistance, and death. . . . That room was where we, a handful of LGBTQ kids in rural America, met to talk openly and safely."

GSAs can be a valuable lifeline at a time in life when many LGBTQ young people feel alienated and lost.

STARTING A GSA

A GSA is a great way to find community right in your own school. Many schools already have GSAs established, but if your school doesn't, you can form your own! The Web site of the GSA Network (gsanetwork.org) offers some advice on how to form a GSA at your school.

1. Follow guidelines. Your school has rules about how clubs are to be formed—make sure you follow them.
2. Find an advisor. You'll need a school staff member, usually a teacher, to act as an advisor for the club. Try to find someone you already know is an ally.

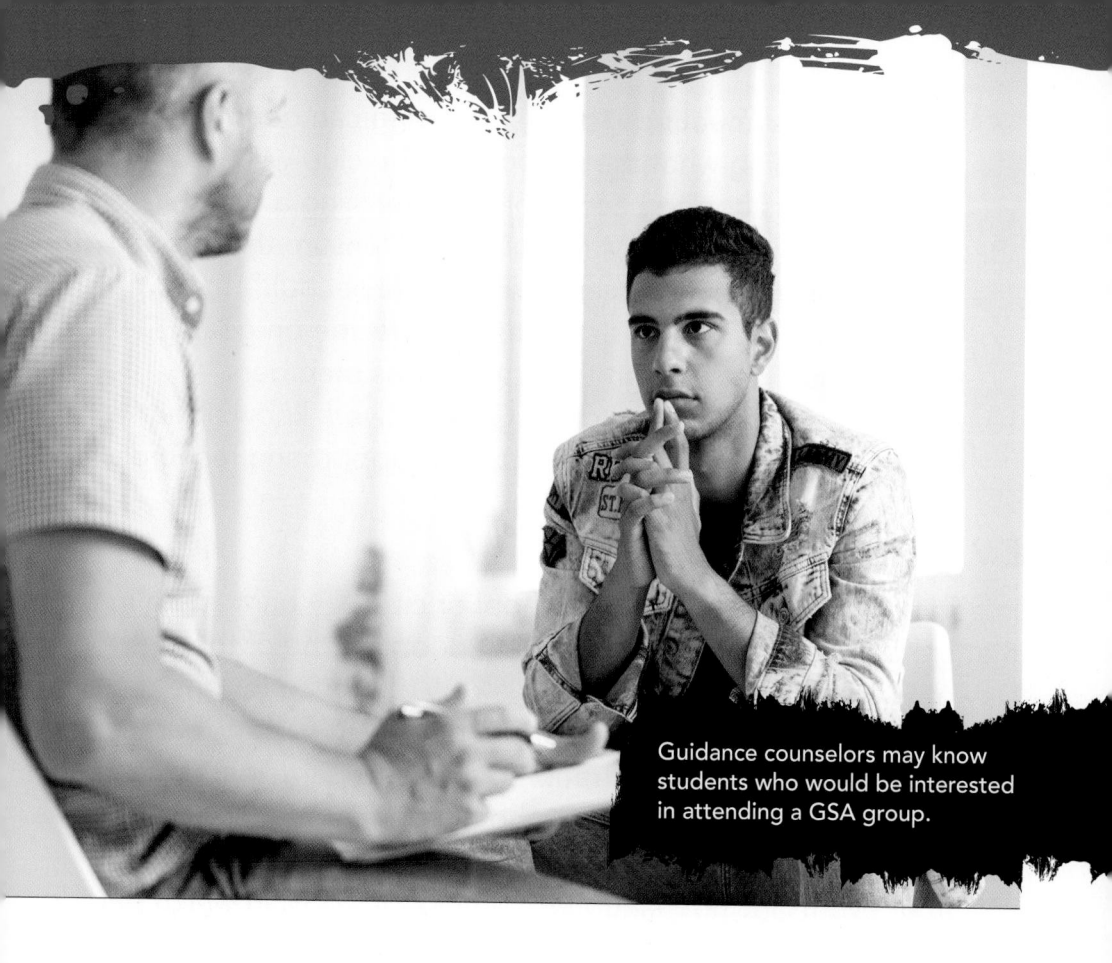

Guidance counselors may know students who would be interested in attending a GSA group.

3. Inform your administration of your plans. Hopefully, this will smooth the way for forming the club, allowing them to support you as to any obstacles you might find. If the administration isn't supportive, the GSA network says, "Let them know that forming a GSA club is legally protected." You can find more information about the legal issues involved on the GSA Web site.

4. Inform guidance counselors about the GSA. They "may know students who would be interested in attending the group."

5. Pick a meeting place. Find a safe place that students can find easily. This is often your advisor's classroom.

6. Advertise (and get food!). Make sure people know that the club meeting is happening, where it's happening, and that there will be food there. "People always come to meetings when you provide food!"

7. Hold your first meeting. The first meeting can be for introductions and for deciding what the purpose of the club will be. What do club members hope to accomplish by forming a GSA?
8. Establish ground rules. Make rules that "ensure that group discussions are safe, confidential, and respectful."
9. Plan for the future. Plan activities, and decide on goals. Decide on specific tasks, and assign them to various members.
10. Register your GSA! Letting the GSA Network know about your club allows them to provide you with support and resources.

EVENTS

In addition to a GSA club, your school or city may participate in events that are geared toward young LGBTQ people. One of these is the Day of Silence, when students take a vow of silence for one day in recognition of the silencing of LGBTQ people in society, particularly in schools. If a school's administration decides to participate, the Day of Silence can be accompanied by school assemblies or special lessons in class to discuss the issue.

Other events include National Coming Out Day, in which people are encouraged to speak openly about their sexual orientation and gender identity in order to encourage greater visibility, and Ally Week, in which other straight students are encouraged to support LGBTQ students in dealing with harassment and bullying.

Another resource you may be able to find in your area, or perhaps even in your school, is GLSEN (pronounced "glisten"), an organization that was created specifically to help K–12 LGBTQ kids in schools across the country. GLSEN sponsors the Day of Silence and provides assistance in forming GSAs.

You should know that although many people find accessing LGBTQ community within their schools helpful in their lives, it's okay not to feel ready to be out of the closet. If you are uncomfortable with being open about your identity, or if you think being open could endanger you, it's okay to wait for the right time to discuss your identity. When you come out should be up to you.

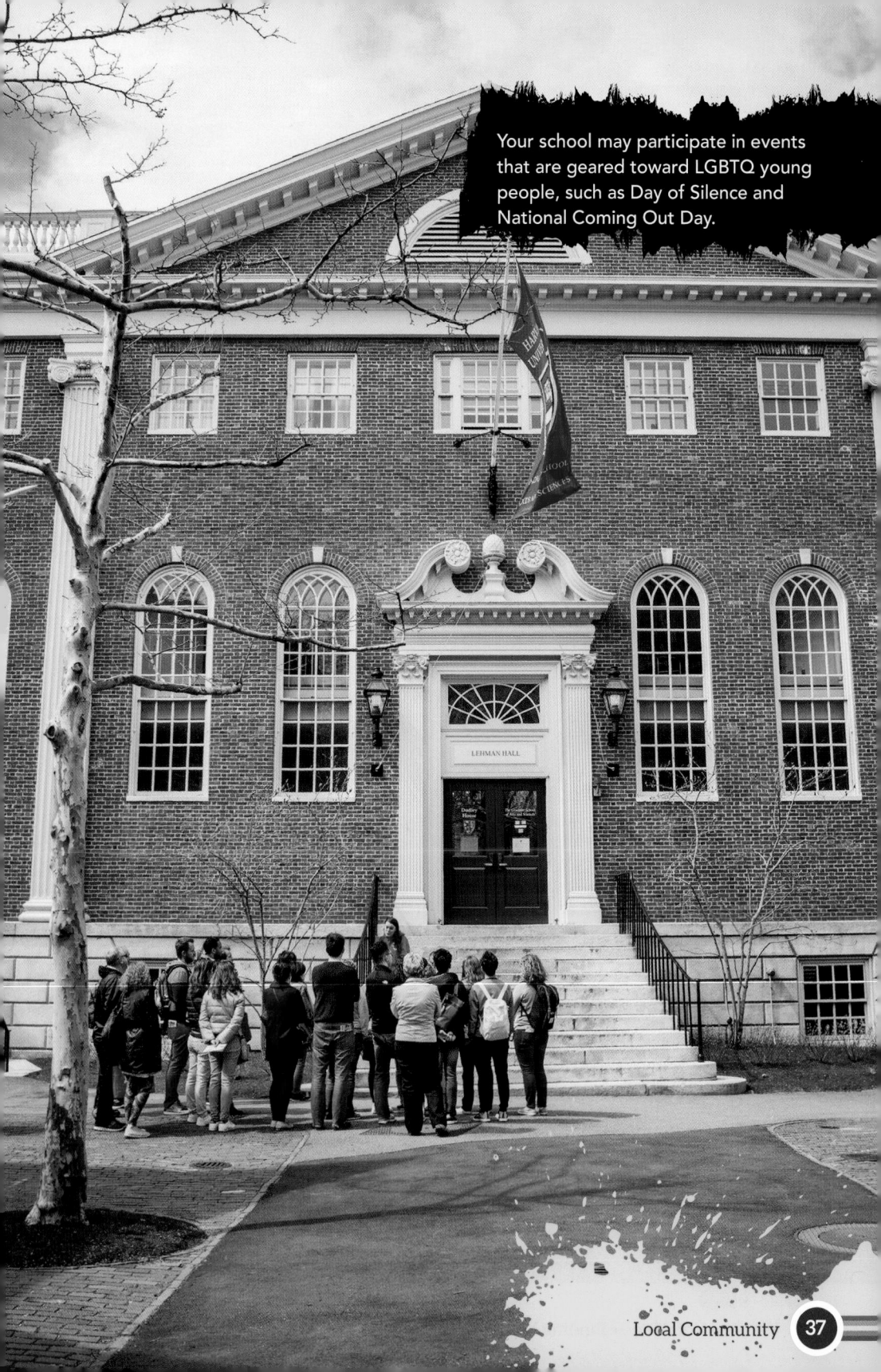

Your school may participate in events that are geared toward LGBTQ young people, such as Day of Silence and National Coming Out Day.

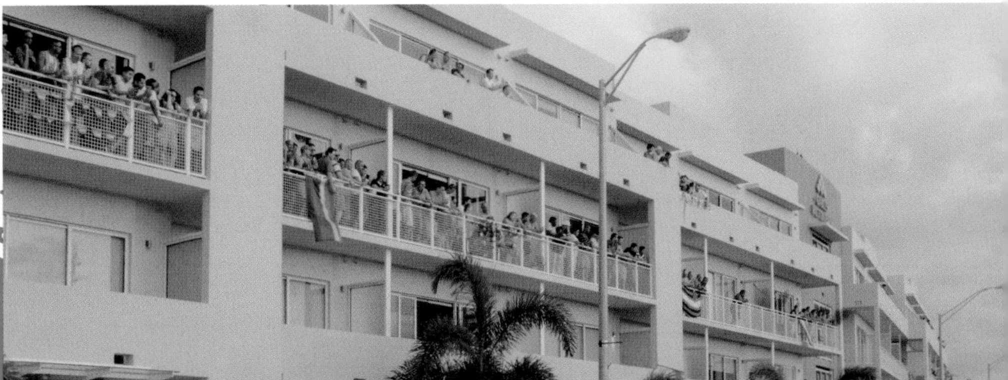

GLSEN was created specifically to help K–12 LGBTQ kids in schools.

THE "GAYBORHOOD"

Some cities have an area that is particularly friendly to LGBTQ businesses, organizations, and homes. An area like this is often referred to as a **gayborhood**, short for "gay neighborhood." These neighborhoods usually contain a number of LGBTQ-oriented businesses like bars, clubs, coffee shops, restaurants, and book stores. A city's LGBTQ community center is also often located within the gayborhood.

Top 10 Things to Do with Your GSA
GLSEN's Ideas for GSA Activities

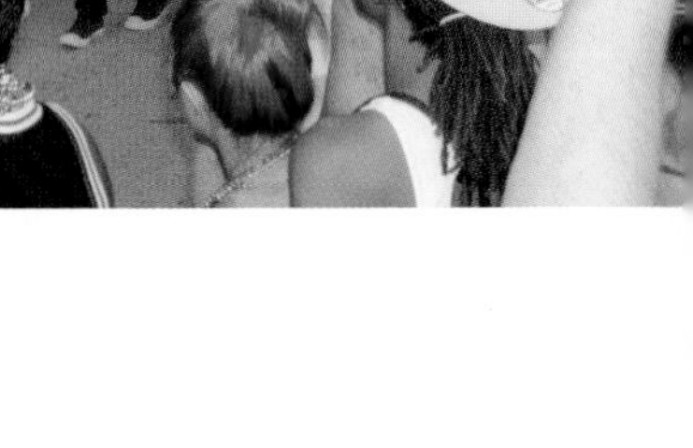

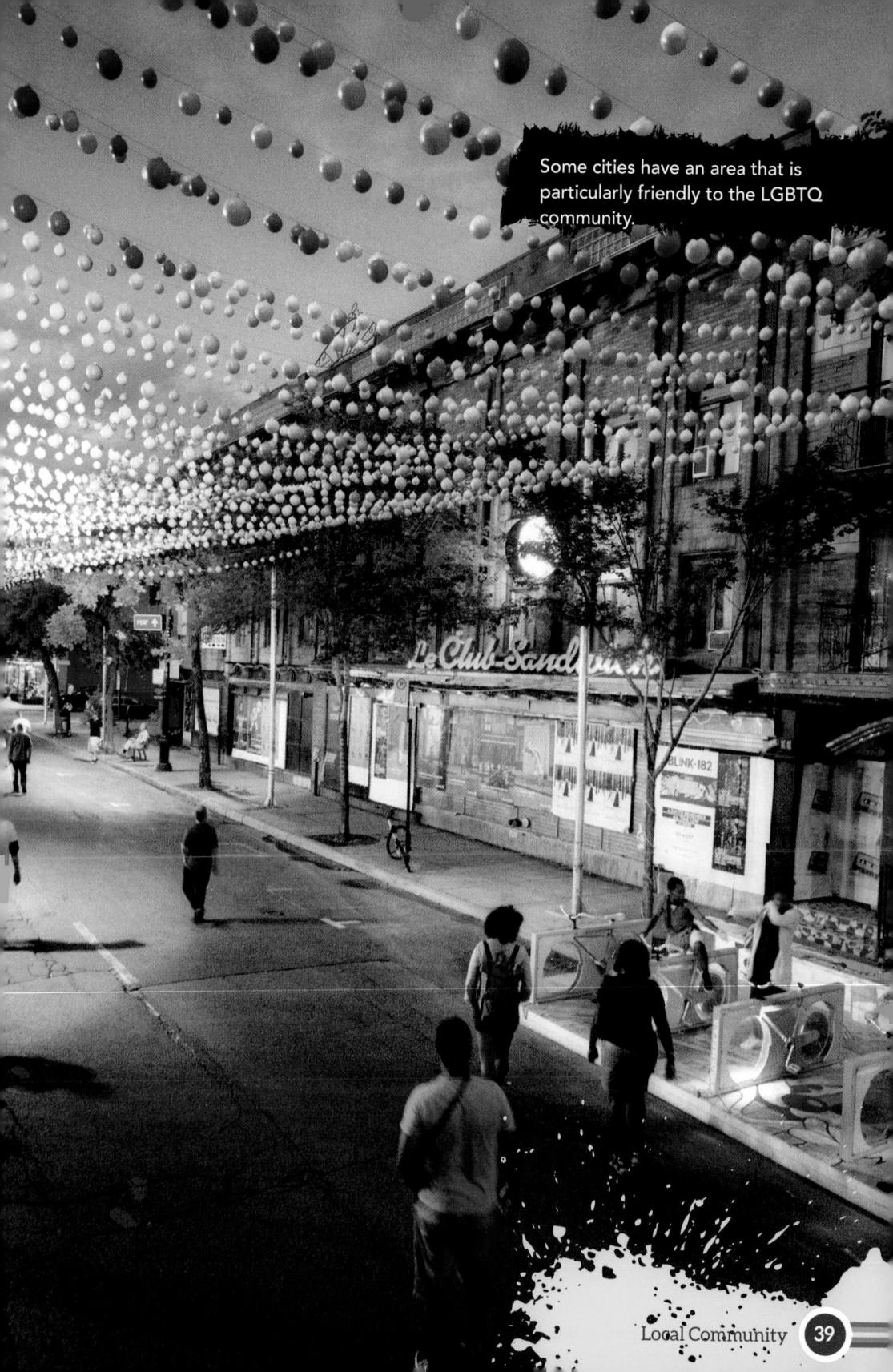

Some cities have an area that is particularly friendly to the LGBTQ community.

Many cities across the country have some form of a community center, which can look very different from place to place. Most offer sexual health services. Many provide services especially meant for youth. Other things a community center might provide are a drug- and alcohol-free hangout space, information about mental health services, support groups, opportunities for political and volunteer involvement, and information about other social opportunities like clubs and sports teams. To find your local community center, check out www.lgbtcenters.org/LGBTCenters.

OTHER WAYS OF FINDING COMMUNITY NEAR YOU

There are many ways that LGBTQ people are able to find people to support them. For some, their church can provide good support by helping them feel accepted in an environment that is not always welcoming to LGBTQ people. (Unfortunately, this isn't an option for everyone.) Others find community through sports, theater, music groups, and any number of other groups and activities. Community doesn't have to be a formal group or organization either, or even specifically meant for LGBTQ people. It can just be your group of friends. Close friends, both LGBTQ and straight, can be some of the best communities that we can have. Straight people who are supportive of LGBTQ rights and individuals are called **allies**. Having allies in your life can be a huge support.

For some LGBTQ people their church can provide valuable support.

ALL ARE WELCOM

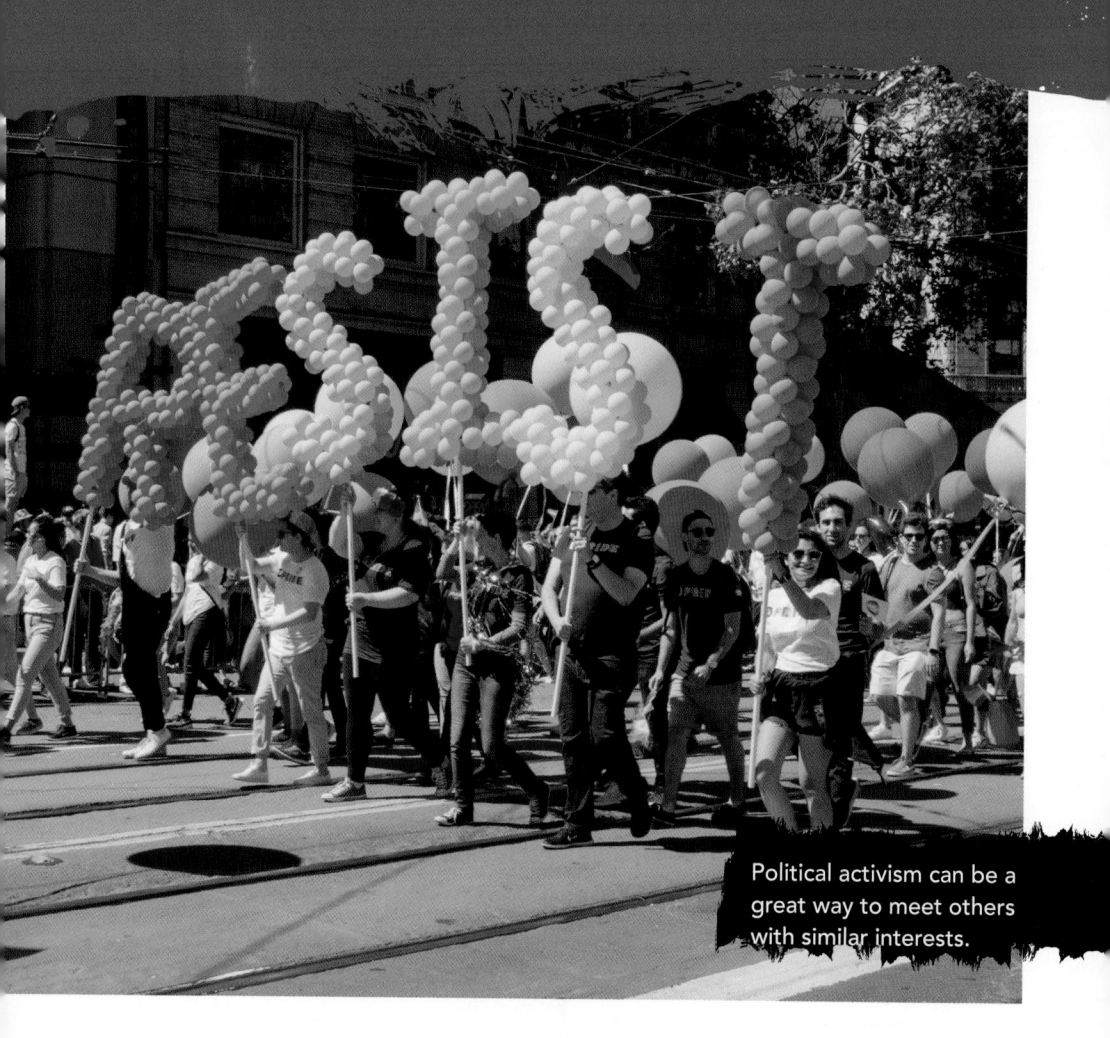

Political activism can be a great way to meet others with similar interests.

Political activism can be a great way to meet others with similar interests and experiences. Finding an LGBTQ-rights organization in your area is a way to get involved, make a difference, and find community in the process. It doesn't have to be just LGBTQ, either. Joining others who are passionate about anything you're passionate about is an affirming experience that can lead to community.

Your family can also serve as a part of your community. If you are lucky enough to have family supportive of you in your sexuality and gender identity, they can fill the same type of role in your life. Many cities have local chapters of PFLAG (Parents and Friends of Lesbians and Gays), which is an organization that was founded in 1973, specifically for families and allies of LGBTQ people to advocate

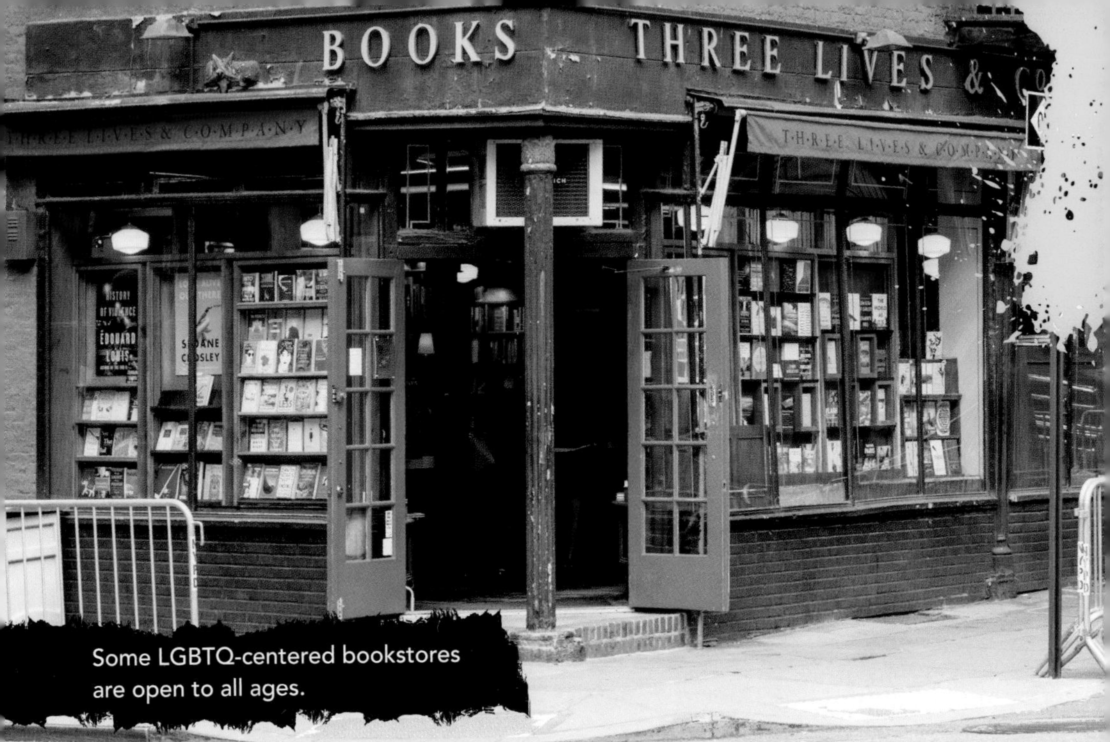

Some LGBTQ-centered bookstores are open to all ages.

for issues important to their family members. If your parents or other family members are supportive, you may want to provide them with the information on your local chapter.

Visiting the Gayborhood While Underage

Visiting the gayborhood can be a little tricky while underage because a lot of the businesses are aimed toward adults. Bars and clubs, of course, are inaccessible to younger people. Some bookstores are also meant for adult customers. Here are a few tips for visiting the gayborhood while under 18:

1. Coffee shops are generally open to all ages.
2. Restaurants are usually open to all ages during meal times. Some become adult-only late at night, but during dinner or before should be safe.
3. Some LGBTQ-centered bookstores are open to all ages. Just call before and ask, or if you're already there, just check for signs. If it's meant only for adults, there should be a sign that says so.
4. If in doubt, call ahead. It never hurts just to ask.
5. Visit your local community center.

TEXT-DEPENDENT QUESTIONS

1. What types of things are likely to be found in a "gayborhood"?

2. What does GSA stand for? How has its meaning changed over time?

3. What LGBTQ-oriented events do schools sometimes participate in?

RESEARCH PROJECTS

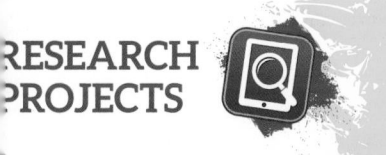

1. Do some research online about the LGBTQ community resources available in your area. Things to look for include community centers, GSAs, gay businesses, and political organizations.

2. Brainstorm some ideas for GSA activities. What types of activities do you think your school would most benefit from? Is there a specific need the students at your school have?

Just a Click Away: Online Community

WORDS TO UNDERSTAND

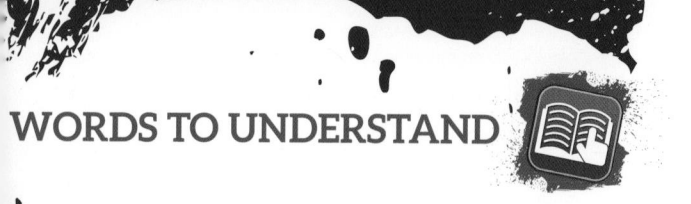

ANONYMITY: *Being able to participate in something, like social media, without others knowing who you are.*

CIVIC ENGAGEMENT: *Being involved in a group or activity that is trying to make a difference on a social or political issue.*

SOCIAL MEDIA: *Web sites and apps that allow users to create online communities to share information, personal messages, and more.*

On September 21, 2010, writer and radio personality Dan Savage, together with his boyfriend (now husband) Terry Miller, posted a video to YouTube. Deeply concerned about a rise in suicides among young LGBTQ people who had been victims of bullying, the couple decided to do something about it. In the video, Dan and Terry share their experiences growing up in communities and families that did not support them in their sexual orientation. They described the bullying they had experienced growing up. And they told the world how things had changed for them when they became adults and were able to live their lives as they chose. They coined the phrase "it gets better" and started a movement.

In the years since then, more than 50,000 people have shared stories of surviving their tough childhood and adolescence in

More than 50,000 people have shared stories of surviving adolescence in "It Gets Better" videos.

"It Gets Better" videos. People of all sexual orientations and gender identities—everyone from RuPaul, Ellen DeGeneres, professional basketball player Jason Collins, Laverne Cox, *Star Trek* actor George Takei, Rosie O'Donnell, and President Barack Obama to a whole lot of regular, everyday people—have shared messages of support for LGBTQ youth. The purpose of the movement from that first video post has been to show kids and young adults that they are not alone. Many others have suffered the same harassment and come through it stronger with lives they are happy to be living.

"It Gets Better" is one of the greatest examples of the Internet's power to inspire millions of people all over the world—videos on the site have been viewed more than 50 million times. Thanks to "It Gets Better," LGBTQ kids everywhere have access to personal messages from people who understand what they're going through and can offer sympathy and encouragement. But this is just one example of a way to find community online.

"It Gets Better" is one of the greatest examples of the Internet's power to inspire millions of people.

It Gets Better
Dan and Terry—the video that started it all.

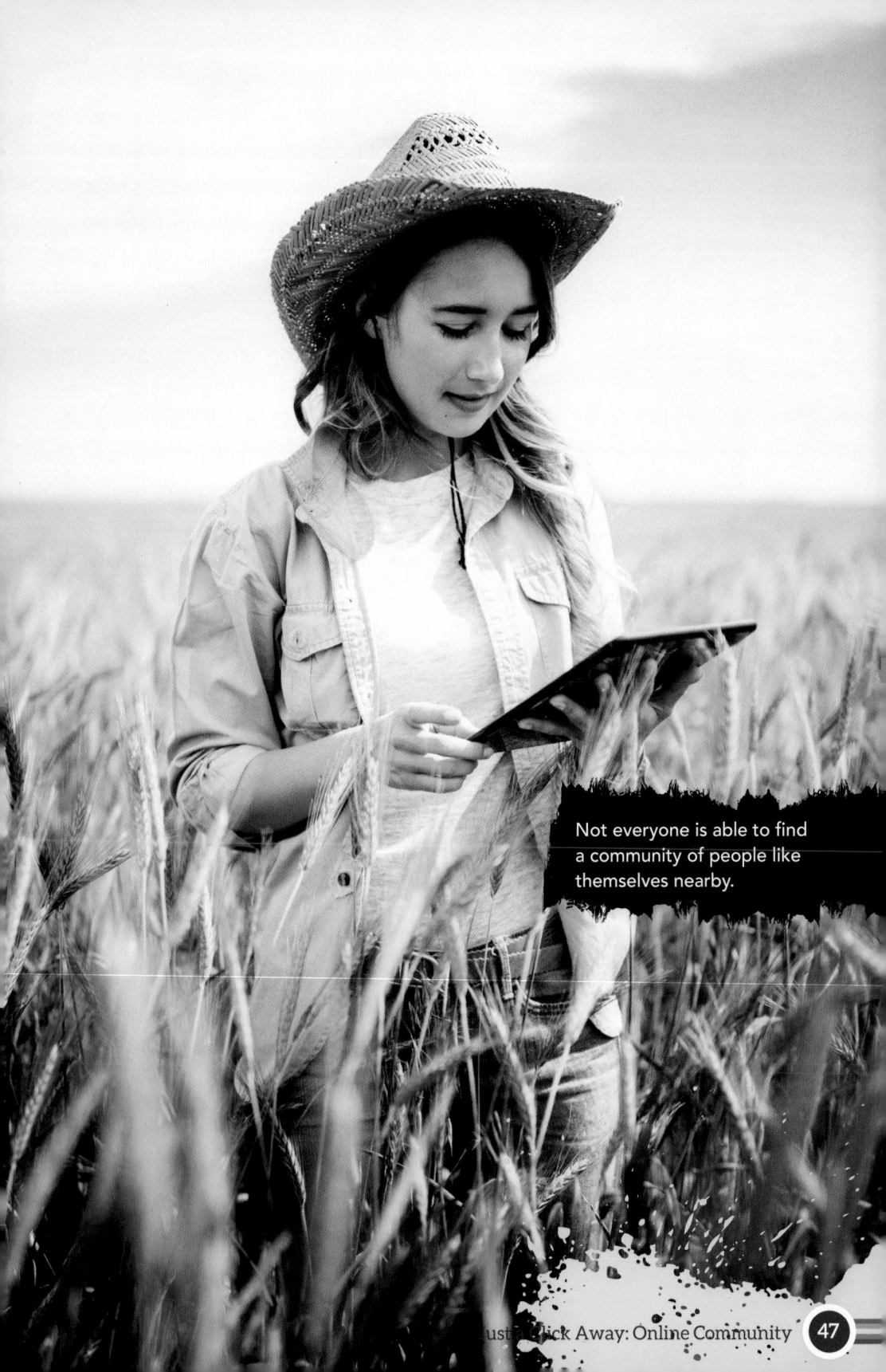

Not everyone is able to find a community of people like themselves nearby.

THE POWER OF THE INTERNET

Unfortunately, not everyone is able to find a community of people like themselves nearby. They might live in an area where no resources exist for LGBTQ people. Where they live, it might be difficult or dangerous to even seek the resources they need. For these people and many others, online community can provide the same support that local communities do.

Even for those who *do* have a local community, the Internet provides a bigger, more diverse network of people who can reassure them that many others feel as they do. And for people who are still figuring out how they identify, the Internet can be a great source of information and guidance. According to research conducted by GLSEN, two-thirds of LGBTQ youth use the Internet as a way to connect with other LGBTQ people. And more than half of them said that they were not out in their everyday lives. A large number of the young LGBTQ people surveyed also said that they were more open with online friends than with others in their life.

Two-thirds of LGBTQ youth use the Internet as a way to connect with other LGBTQ people.

Some even said that they had first disclosed their LGBT identity to someone online. The Internet has enabled young people to connect with others like them who share the same struggles and identity issues.

Nichole and Kobi, two young LGBTQ people from Chico, California, used the Internet as part of their own coming-out experiences. Nichole

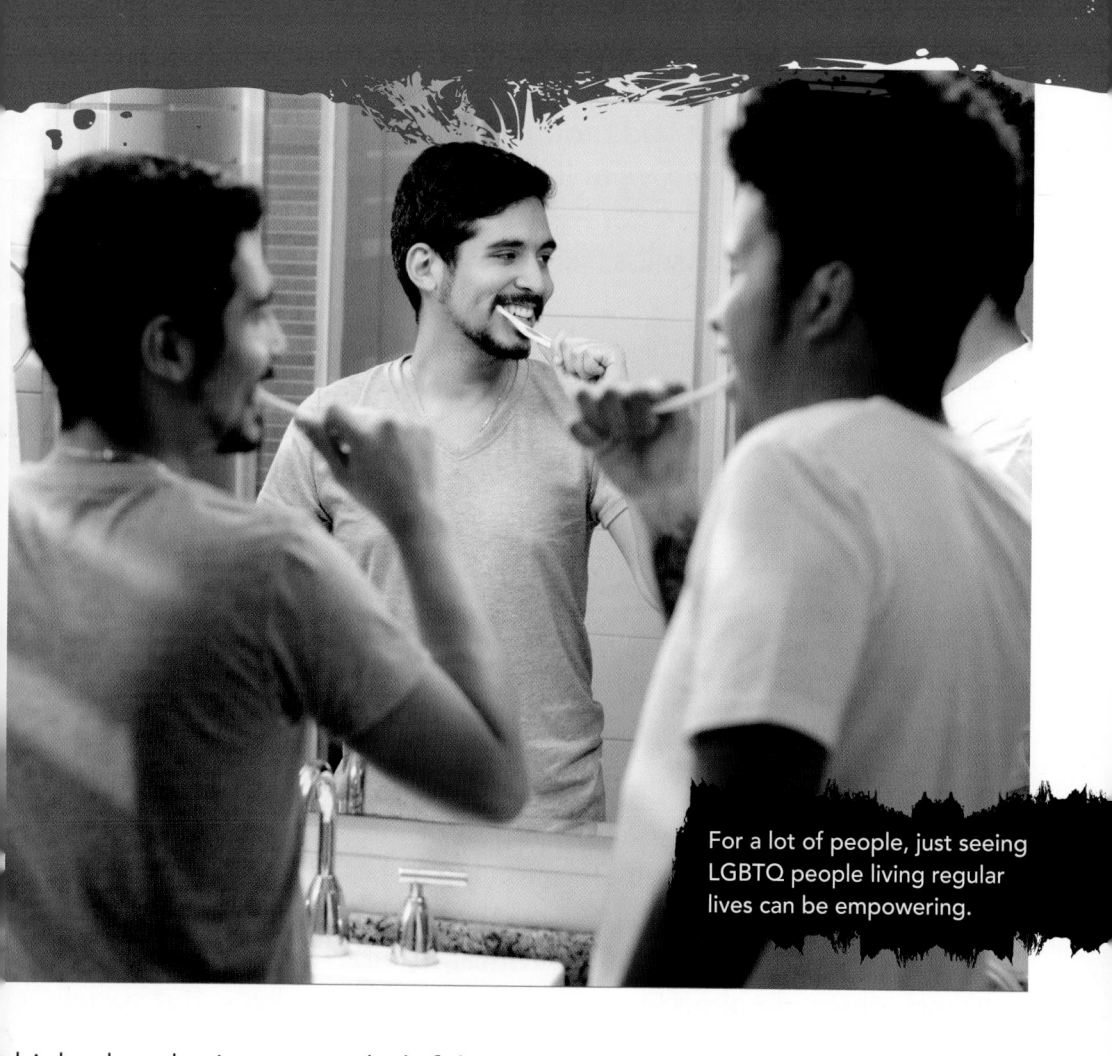

For a lot of people, just seeing LGBTQ people living regular lives can be empowering.

thinks that the Internet is helpful to people just beginning their openly LGBTQ lives because "they can learn the lingo and meet amazing people from all over the globe that they can resonate and connect with and who identify similar to them." Kobi adds, "You're able to confirm what you're feeling."

FINDING EXAMPLES OF LGBTQ LIFE

For a lot of people, just seeing LGBTQ people living regular lives can be empowering. If there aren't openly LGBTQ people around, something as simple as watching an LGBTQ-themed movie on Netflix can help.

The Internet is full of LGBTQ people who offer positive examples of what it's like to be out and proud. Popular vloggers talk about things like their daily lives, what it's like to date as an LGBTQ person, and their own coming-out stories. They share personal details of their breakups, family relationships, school experiences, interests, and other aspects of who they are.

These YouTube stars cover a wide range of personalities; so, chances are good that you can find someone you can relate to. Some of the most popular LGBTQ vloggers are Tyler Oakley, Eva Gutowski, Troye Sivan, Gigi Gorgeous, Davey Wavey, and Hannah Hart. There are many, many more, but even this small sample includes lesbians, gay men, bisexuals, and transgender people. (Nichole's favorite YouTube star is the drag queen Jeffree Star.)

FINDING COMMUNITY ON SOCIAL MEDIA

For isolated LGBTQ youth, **social media** can provide a much-needed connection to others like them all over the world. Being able to talk to people who understand what you are going through can make all the difference. Some even find that an online friend far away understands them better than the people around them do.

Sites and apps like Facebook, Twitter, Tumblr, Snapchat, and a hundred others are already a part of many people's lives. But social media can be much more than entertainment or a time-waster. It can be a tool to help people find their community and feel supported in their lives.

One of the advantages of social media for people who are just starting to figure out their sexuality or gender identity is **anonymity**. For example, a girl who thinks she might be a lesbian can anonymously ask a lesbian on Tumblr for help in figuring it out. She can ask the woman how she knew that she was a lesbian and how she learned to embrace it. A lot of social media, like Tumblr and Twitter, allow a person to be anonymous if they choose to be.

There are many Web sites and apps that allow LGBTQ teens to communicate with each other. Private Facebook groups, for example,

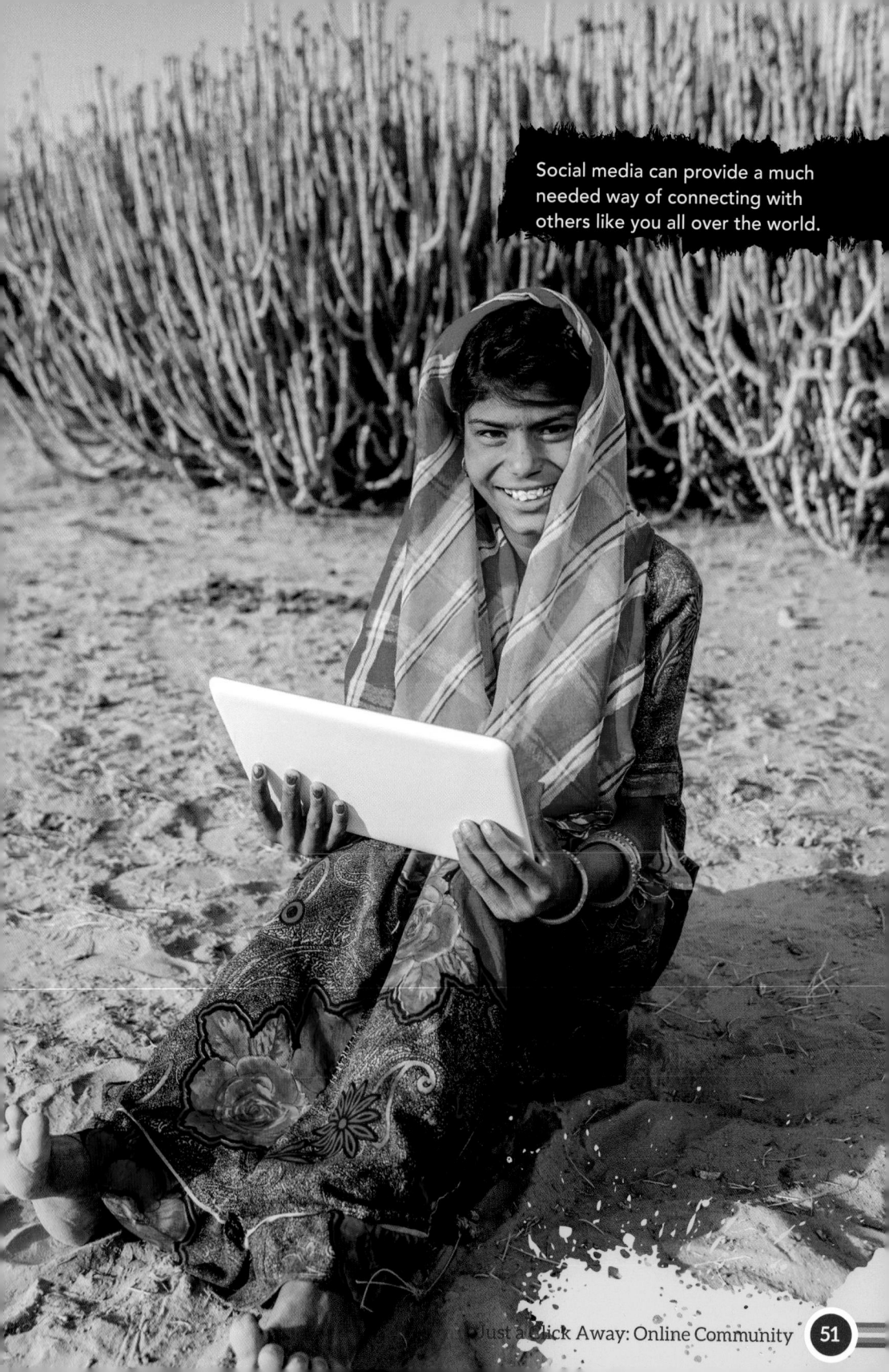

Social media can provide a much needed way of connecting with others like you all over the world.

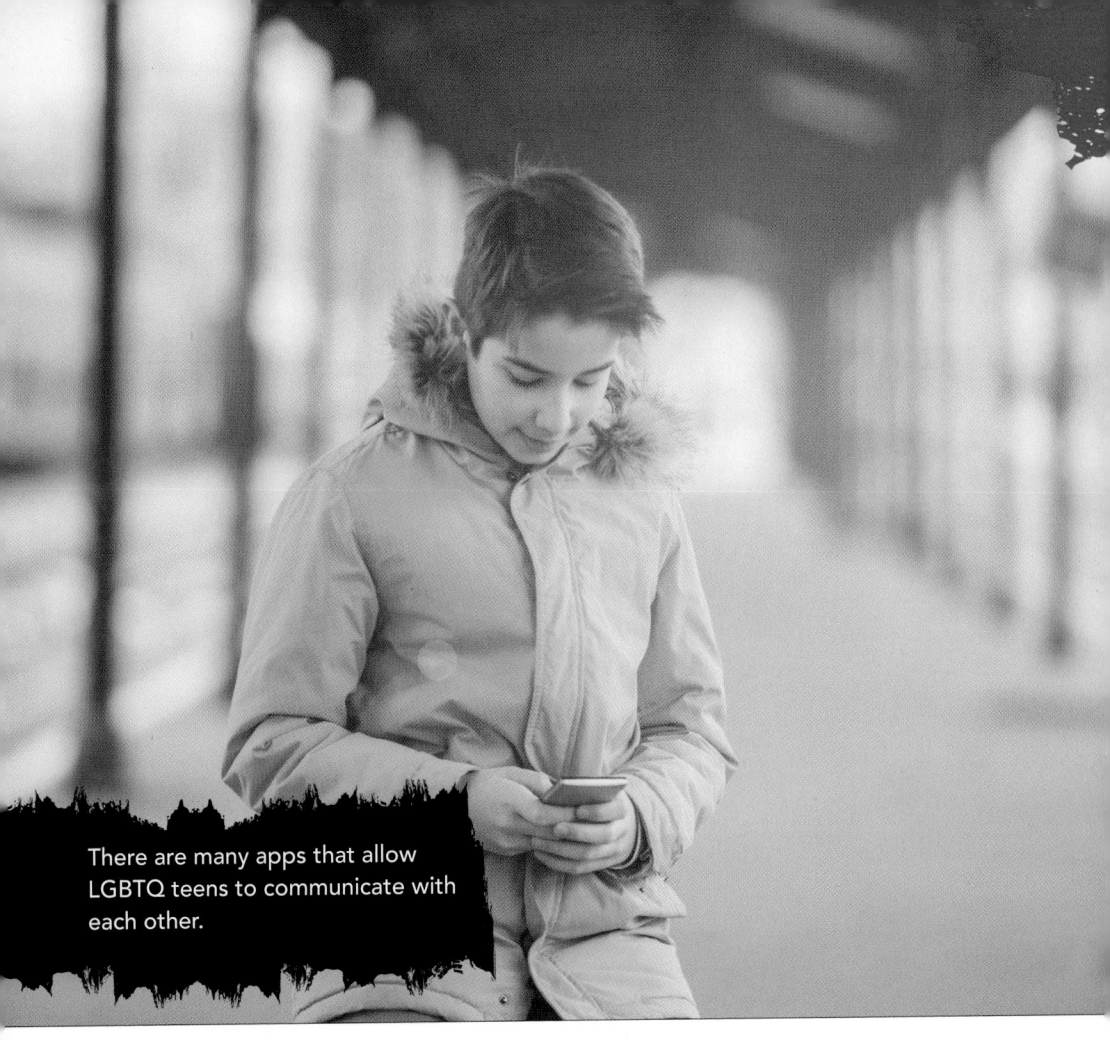

There are many apps that allow LGBTQ teens to communicate with each other.

allow people to chat confidentially—only people in the group can read what they are saying. "There are tens of millions of active groups on Facebook," a Facebook spokesperson told the online magazine *The Daily Dot*. "People in the LGBT community frequently tell us the closed safe space of Facebook groups helps them feel more connected to others." This type of online group can help LGBTQ people discuss what's going on in their lives with friends in confidence.

The many different social media sites and apps that LGBTQ people use to communicate with each other include Reddit, Tumblr, Twitter, and many more. There is even a social media site made specifically for LGBTQ people ages 13 to 24, called TrevorSpace (www.trevorspace.org). It's sort

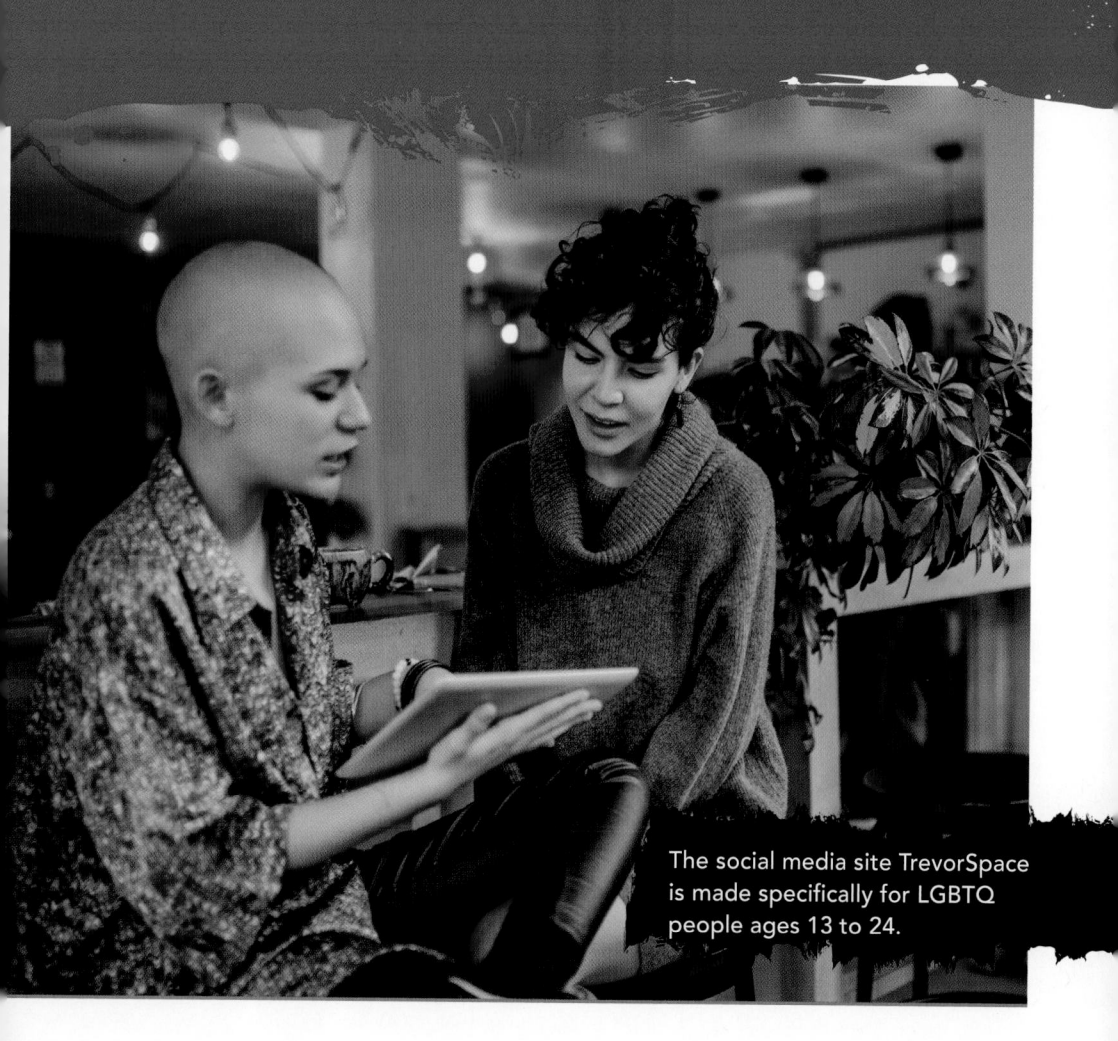

The social media site TrevorSpace is made specifically for LGBTQ people ages 13 to 24.

of a combination of Reddit and Facebook, where young people can safely talk about things that are important to them with others who share similar concerns and experiences.

OTHER WAYS TO USE THE INTERNET

Just as anonymity can be helpful on social media, it can also make other online activities more comfortable. For instance, you can read blogs about LGBTQ subjects without having to come out and announce your sexual orientation or gender identity to the world. It's a way to find out more information about what it means to be LGBTQ before you feel comfortable identifying yourself to others that way.

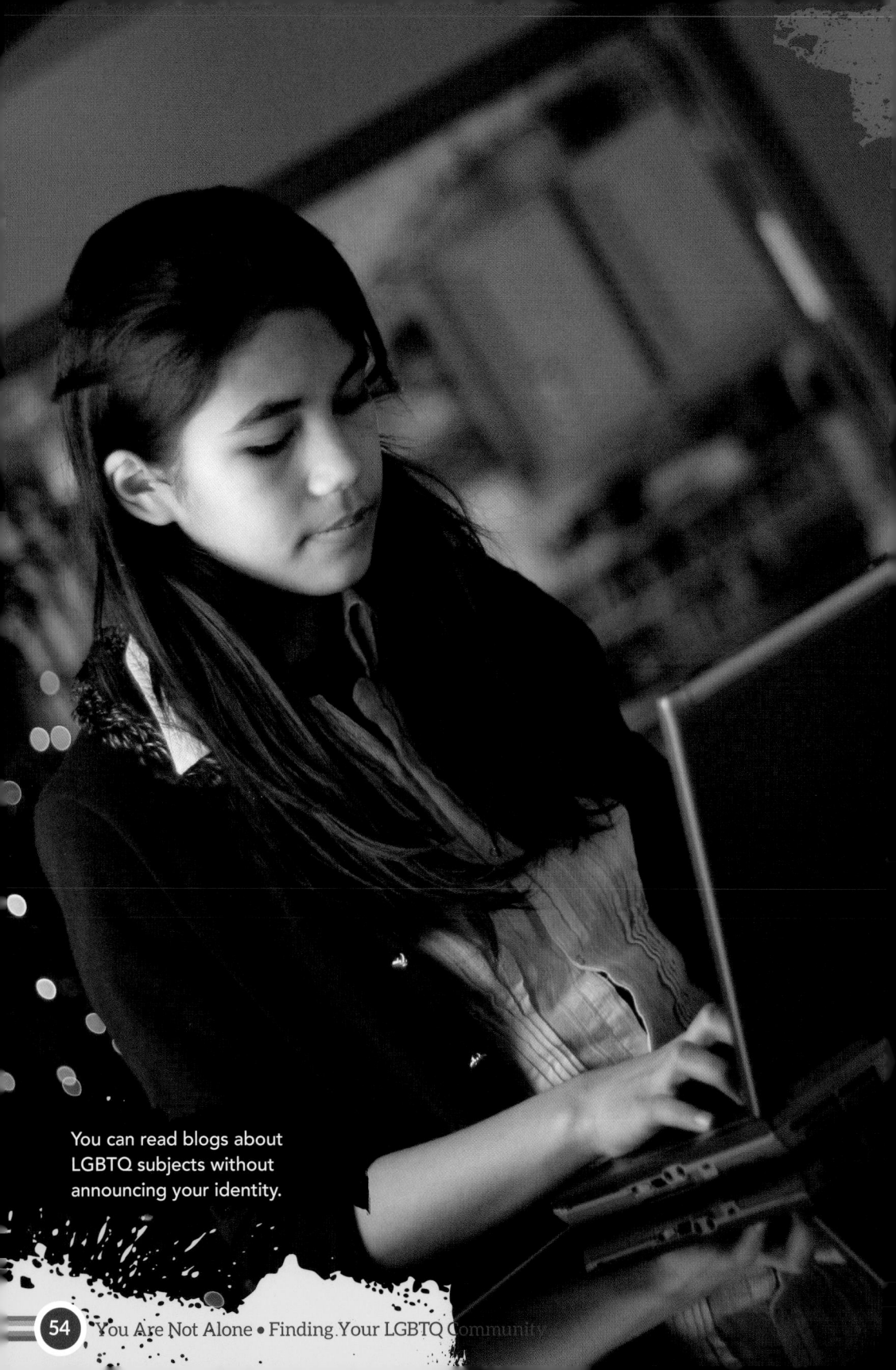

You can read blogs about LGBTQ subjects without announcing your identity.

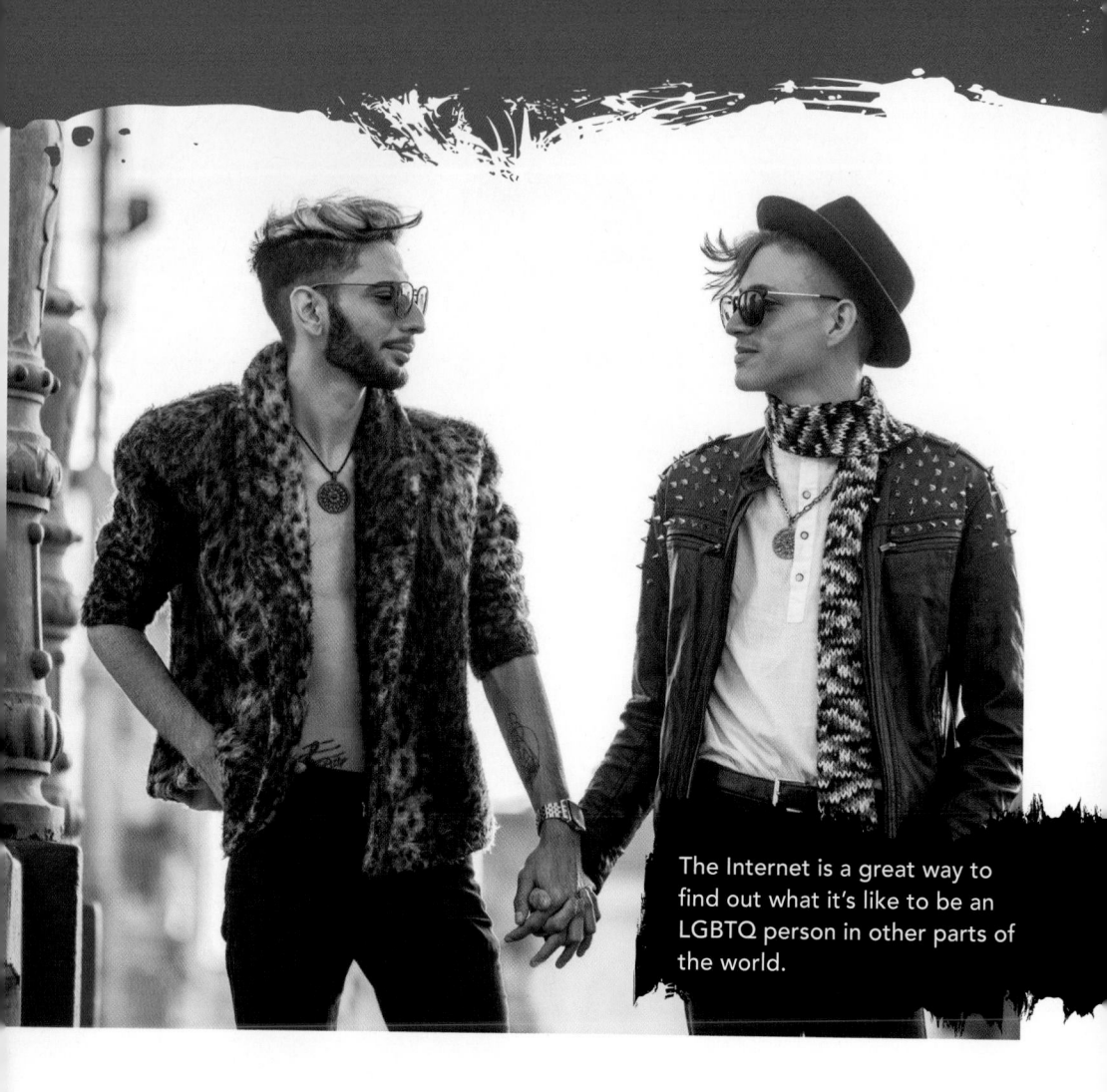

The Internet is a great way to find out what it's like to be an LGBTQ person in other parts of the world.

Some LGBTQ people use the Internet as a tool for **civic engagement**, getting involved in political and social causes. The GLSEN research says that LGBTQ youth are twice as likely to use the Internet for social and political involvement than are other young people. People can use the Internet to join a group that supports a cause or issue. It can be used as a way to get the word out about an issue or to recruit people for an event or activity.

The Internet is also a great way to find out what it's like to be an LGBTQ person in other parts of the world. Using social media to connect with LGBTQ people who live all around the globe is a

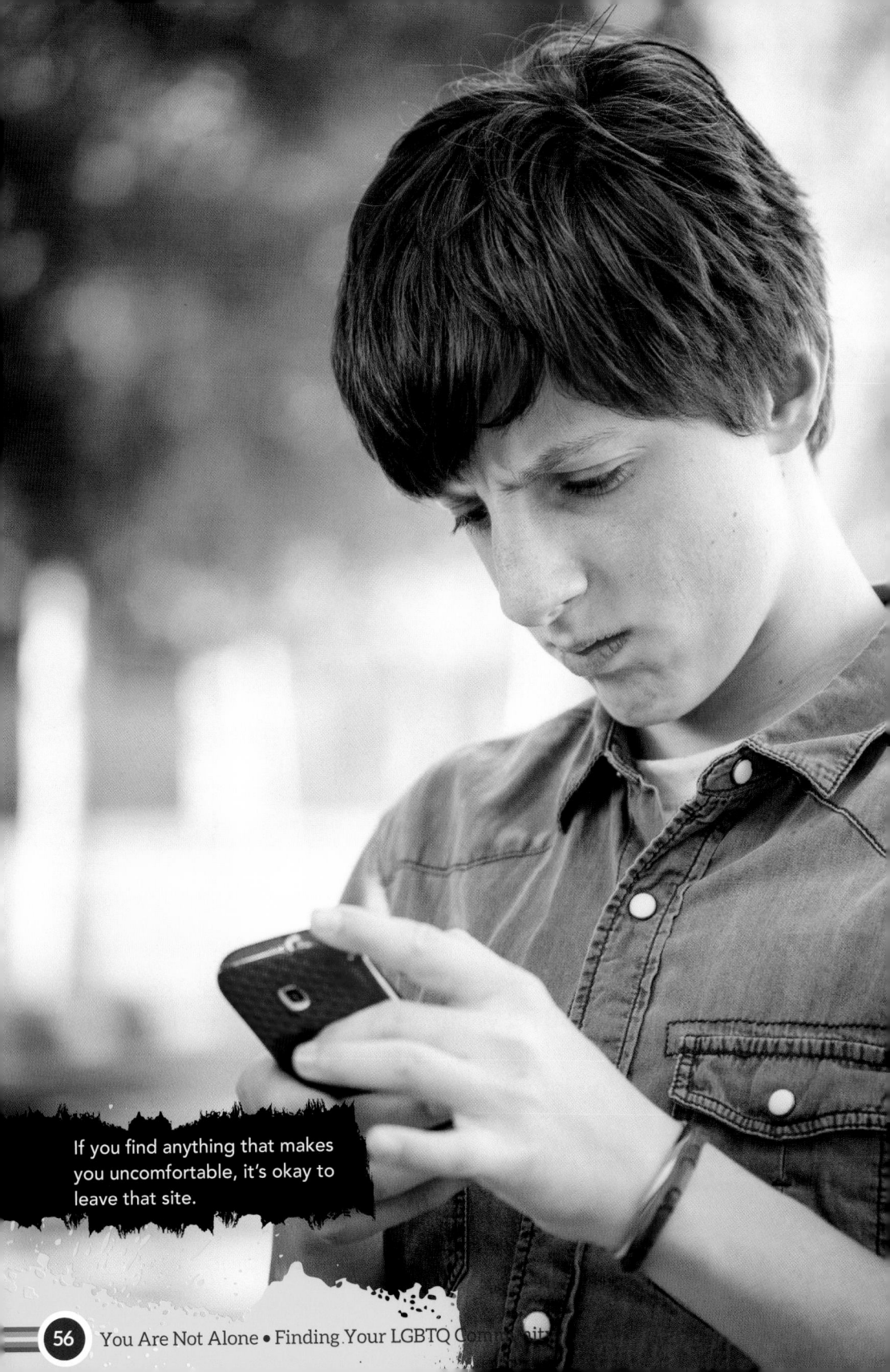

If you find anything that makes you uncomfortable, it's okay to leave that site.

fascinating opportunity. Chatting with foreign online friends and comparing experiences can give you a greater understanding of the world and the wide range of LGBTQ life that exists. Web sites, blogs, and articles that provide information on international LGBTQ issues can also be found.

SAFETY ONLINE AND OFFLINE

In addition to good resources and information, the Internet has a lot of content that isn't appropriate for young people. If you think that something you find is meant for an older person, or you come across anything that makes you uncomfortable, it's always okay to leave that site and find content that better fits you.

While the Internet and social media can be great ways to connect with people who have similar experiences and interests, it's important to stay safe and protect yourself. The ConnectSafely Web site gives advice on how to use the Web in a safe way. "Read between the lines.' It may be fun to check out new people for friendship or romance, but be aware that, while some people are nice, others act nice because they're trying to get something. Flattering or supportive messages may be more about manipulation than friendship or romance."

ConnectSafely also gives advice about meeting people in real life whom you have met online. "Avoid in-person meetings. The only way someone can physically harm you is if you're both in the same location, so—to be 100% safe—don't meet them in person. If you really must get together with someone you 'met' online, don't go alone. Have the meeting in a public place, tell a parent or some other solid backup, and bring some friends along."

Be careful of what people are asking you to send them as well. Never give personal information like addresses to people you have never met. Never send explicit pictures because you don't know how the other person might use them. For people under 18, sending personal details may also create legal problems.

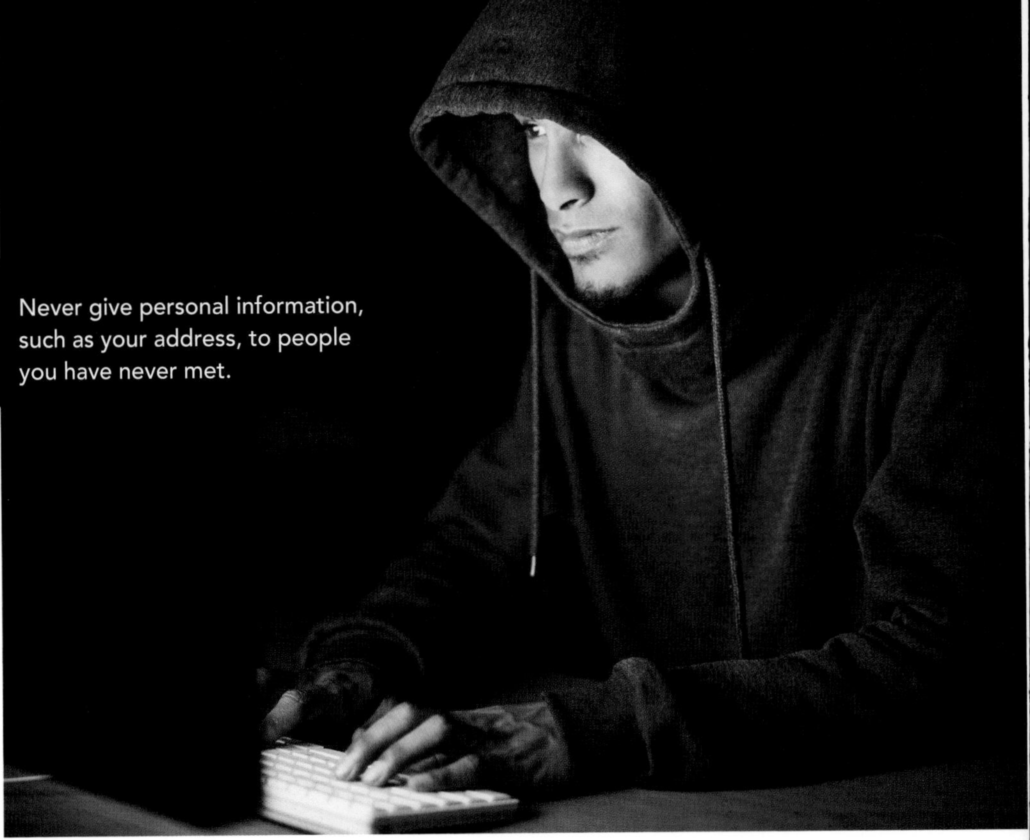

Never give personal information, such as your address, to people you have never met.

Online Help for Mental Health

For people who are having a hard time dealing with their sexuality, gender identity, or any other part of life, there are resources online to help. The Trevor Project is a group that was created specifically to help young LGBTQ people through what can be a very difficult period in their lives. It has been filling that role for 20 years now. The Trevor Project now provides help over the phone, text, and online chat. It also operates the social media network TrevorSpace, though the two services are separate. There is more information about what it does at www.thetrevorproject.org/get-help-now/. If you find yourself having thoughts about suicide, get help now.

Another resource that can help is 7 Cups of Tea (www.7cups.com), which describes itself as "the world's largest emotional support system." Though it isn't exclusively for LGBTQ people, it does have some resources specifically for them, and some of their trained "active listeners" specialize in LGBTQ issues.

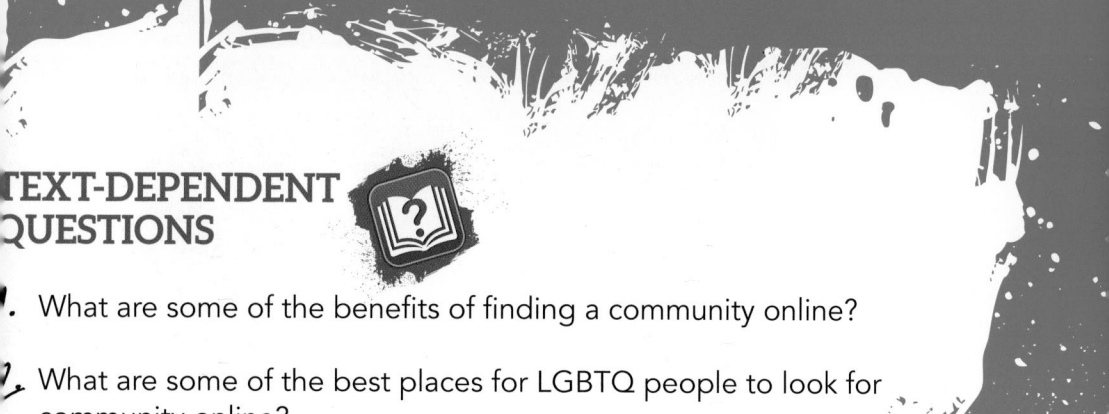

TEXT-DEPENDENT QUESTIONS

1. What are some of the benefits of finding a community online?

2. What are some of the best places for LGBTQ people to look for community online?

3. What are some mental health resources that are available online?

4. What are some of the precautions a person should take while interacting with others online?

RESEARCH PROJECTS

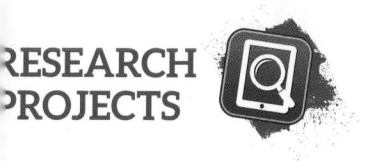

1. Watch six to eight videos on the "It Gets Better" Web site (www.itgetsbetterproject.org). Are there experiences and feelings that they have in common? Are there experiences that are different for each one? Are there some stories you can relate to more than others?

2. Watch some videos by openly LGBTQ YouTube personalities. Find one that you especially relate to. What is it about it that speaks to you personally?

3. Try to make an online friend. Use social media to find someone you can relate to and reach out to them. It can be as simple as commenting on a post. If you feel comfortable enough, you could try sending a message explaining your situation and what you're going through.

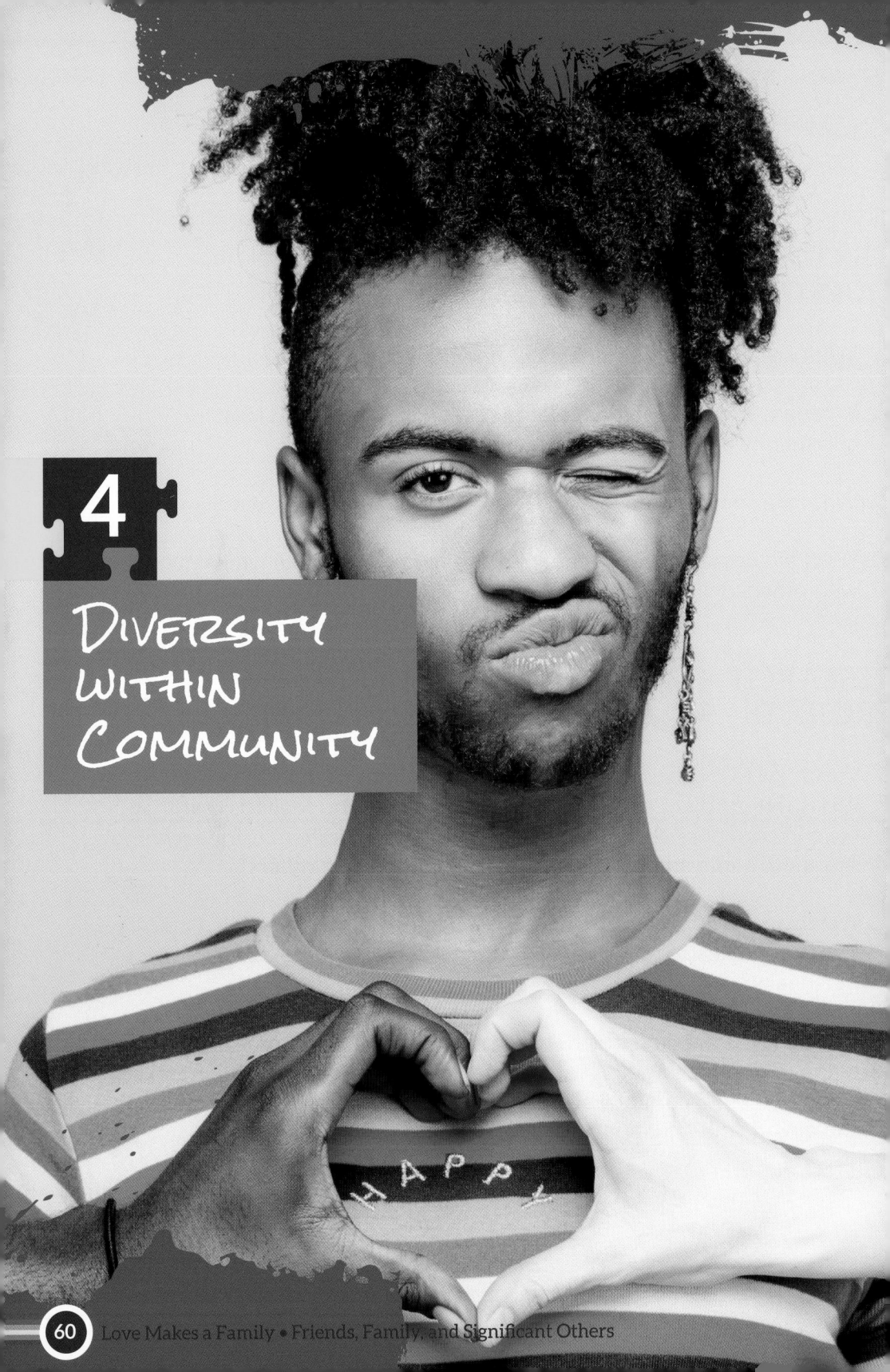

4

DIVERSITY WITHIN COMMUNITY

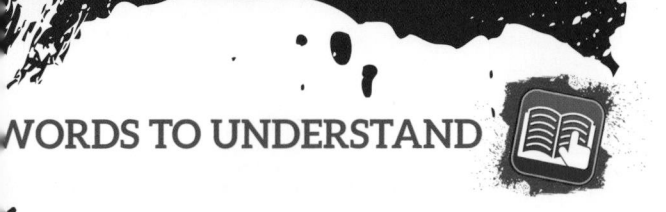

WORDS TO UNDERSTAND

GENDER-NEUTRAL: *When you refer to someone without indicating whether they are male or female.*

LATINX: *A gender-neutral or non-binary way to refer to people or the culture that would otherwise be referred to as Latino or Latina.*

QUEER STUDIES: *The study of what it means to be queer, as well as the study of other fields from an LGBTQ perspective.*

Our sexual orientation and gender identity are important parts of who we are, but they are not the only parts of us that determine *what kind of person* we are. For all of us, it the combination of our many traits that makes us who we are. Sometimes having a different combination of identities from those that are around makes a person feel special and unique, but sometimes it can make a person feel isolated or out of place as well.

As Spenser Clark wrote in *Out Sports* on the subject of being black and gay, "Being a double minority has its great moments, but also its drawbacks when the two groups don't see eye to eye. . . . Many times I feel outcast with the homophobia that exists in the black community because black men are taught that you have to be tough, you have to be brave, you have to get the girl to prove your worth. Being gay is seen as being weak, and being weak is unacceptable. That mindset has to be dissolved into a community where all members are accepted as valid."

But just as those who share Clark's racial identity don't always understand his sexual identity, those who share his sexual identity sometimes don't understand his racial identity. "It is no different in the LGBT community, where racism still runs rampant." No community is flawless, and the LGBTQ community certainly has room to grow.

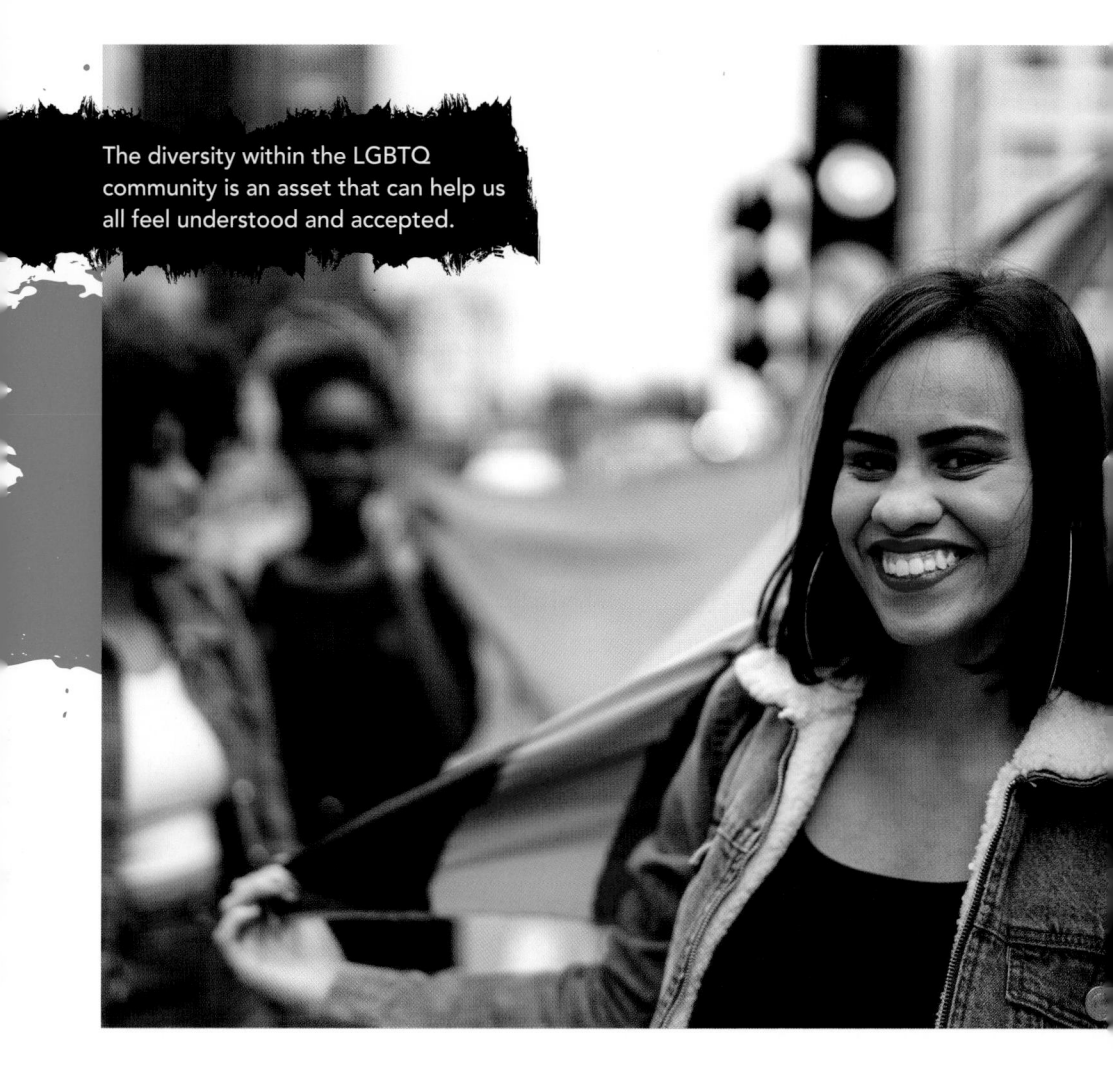

The diversity within the LGBTQ community is an asset that can help us all feel understood and accepted.

But the diversity within the community is an asset that has the potential to help us all feel understood and accepted. Don't ever assume that another part of your identity makes you incompatible with finding community with LGBTQ people. These assumptions rely upon stereotypes of what LGBTQ people *can* be. Whether it is an ethnic or cultural identity, religion, or just interests and personality type, there are LGBTQ people you can relate to and find community with.

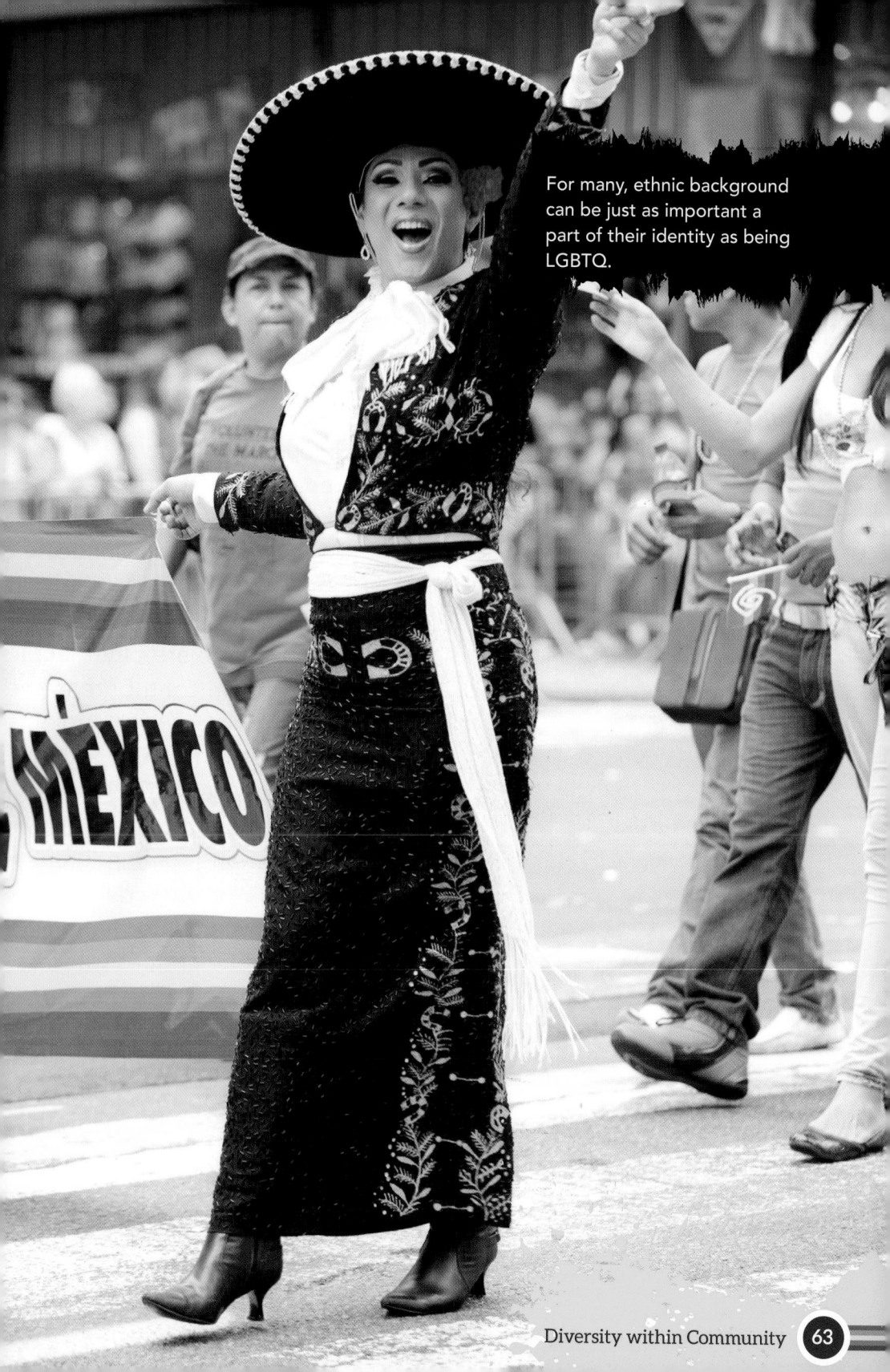

For many, ethnic background can be just as important a part of their identity as being LGBTQ.

ETHNIC DIVERSITY AND COMMUNITY

For many people, their ethnic and cultural background can be just as important a part of their identity as being LGBTQ. For many people of color, this can create a tension between the culture they were raised in and their sexual and gender identity. As the Human Rights Campaign (HRC) points out, for members of many minority communities, "The coming out process can be even more complex to navigate. Often, it requires a unique approach that can cut across multiple languages, cultures, nationalities, religious identities and family generations." Finding a community that understands these unique challenges can be especially helpful in these situations.

Many organizations exist that focus on creating community for minority LGBTQ people.

There are other factors that can contribute to the complexity of multiple levels of identity. HRC points out that "This process can be especially challenging for immigrant parents who were raised in places where information about LGBTQ identities was less widely available. It can be further exacerbated by language barriers that make it challenging to directly translate LGBTQ terminology or make it impossible to find equivalent words to describe LGBTQ identities and experiences."

Fortunately, there are many resources available to people who are facing these unique challenges. Many organizations exist that focus

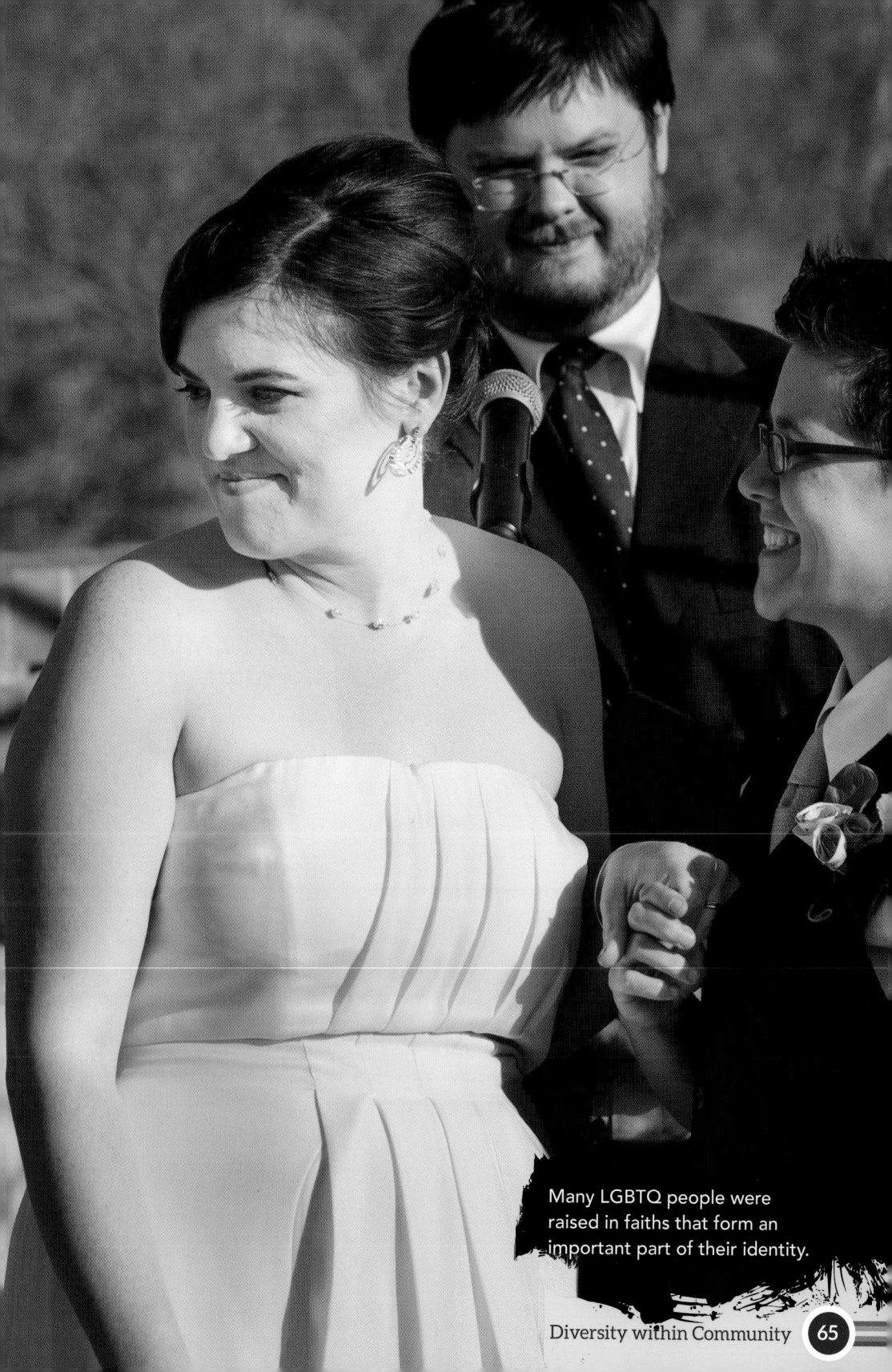

Many LGBTQ people were raised in faiths that form an important part of their identity.

on creating community for minority LGBTQ people. There are even pride celebrations meant specifically for ethnic minorities, for example, Black Pride and **Latinx** Pride celebrations. Sometimes it's as simple as just finding friends who have a similar background. "As you choose to come out and live authentically in your own way, you may find it helpful to surround yourself with others who recognize and affirm your identities," HRC advises. "Many LGBTQ people, including those who may not find full support among our families or communities of heritage, find love and support from 'chosen family,' who fully embrace us for who we are."

There are many faith communities out there that will accept you for who you are.

COMMUNITIES OF FAITH

Just like many other people, many LGBTQ people were raised in faiths that form an important part of their belief system and identity. Unfortunately, there is often tension between religion and the LGBTQ believers. Many have felt persecuted and ostracized by their faith community. While that is changing slowly, not everyone is changing with the culture.

Certain closed-minded religious people try to make it seem like being LGBTQ and being spiritual are not compatible. This is simply no

the case. There are many LGBTQ people for whom spirituality and/or religion continues to be an integral part of their identity even after they begin to live openly with their sexual or gender identity.

For John Caleb Collins, finding a church that was LGBTQ-inclusive while in high school in Mesa, Arizona, meant a lot, even though he was not out of the closet at the time. "Belonging to the church was meaningful to me and was a key supporting group in my life," he says. He has since gone on to earn a master of divinity degree from Fuller Theological Institute and is currently a postulant in the Episcopal Church as an out gay man.

John has some advice for those seeking an LGBTQ-inclusive church. "I would say to follow your heart. Listen to your instincts, and do not settle for just being tolerated," he said. "There are so many faith communities who will accept you for who you are and acknowledge the divine image within you just as you are as a rainbow child of God. . . . For example, there are LGBTQ-affirming networks within the Episcopal Church, Evangelical Lutheran Church in America, Presbyterian Church (USA), Reform Judaism, Unitarian Universalist Association, and the United Methodist Church." These are just a few ideas. There are groups within most churches and faith communities now who are LGBTQ inclusive—some churches are even formed specifically for LGBTQ people!

The point is, your sexual orientation and gender identity are independent of whether you are religious, spiritual, agnostic, or atheist. You may decide to search for community within church, or you may not, but the choice is yours to make.

Holler If You Hear Me: Black and Gay in the Church, a BET special.

DIVERSITY IN INTERESTS

One common stereotype of LGBTQ people involves their areas of interest. Some people believe that gay men are interested in certain specific things, such as fashion and the arts and that lesbians are interested in certain other things, such as sports and cats, to the exclusion of anything else. Though some LGBTQ people do, in fact, enjoy those things—and that's great!—you needn't be limited by any expectations. Whatever your interests may be, you can find other LGBTQ people to share them with. Here are just a few examples:

Sports. The team-oriented nature of many sports lends itself well to forming community. Many people find themselves forming strong bonds with their teammates. Though it's not always so, many young athletes find that those bonds persist after coming out and being open with their team. Hunter Sigmund, from St. Louis, Missouri, found this to be the case "I realize that there are many stigmas surrounding gay athletes, so coming out to my varsity swim and dive team seemed daunting. However, before I even had the chance to tell my teammates many of them approached me and pulled me aside to assure me of their unconditional support," he said, writing in *Out Sports*. It was the support of the high school football captain, who was openly gay and later became his boyfriend, that gave him the courage to do so. This community of both LGBTQ and allied fellow athletes helped him know

The team-oriented nature of many sports lends itself well to forming community.

that he was accepted and valued.

Gaming. When LGBTQ people come to mind, people probably don't think of gaming. But like most things out there, if you look for it, you can find someone who shares your sexual and gender identity who is interested in what you're interested in. One group of three friends found this to be true when they started a group for gay gamers—or "gaymers"—in their home city. One of the founders, named Kristof, told gamesradar.com that since the wider gaming community can be hostile to LGBTQ people, "We are providing a space where people can play without worrying about those things. Some people have to hide their identity because of their background, but they can be open here."

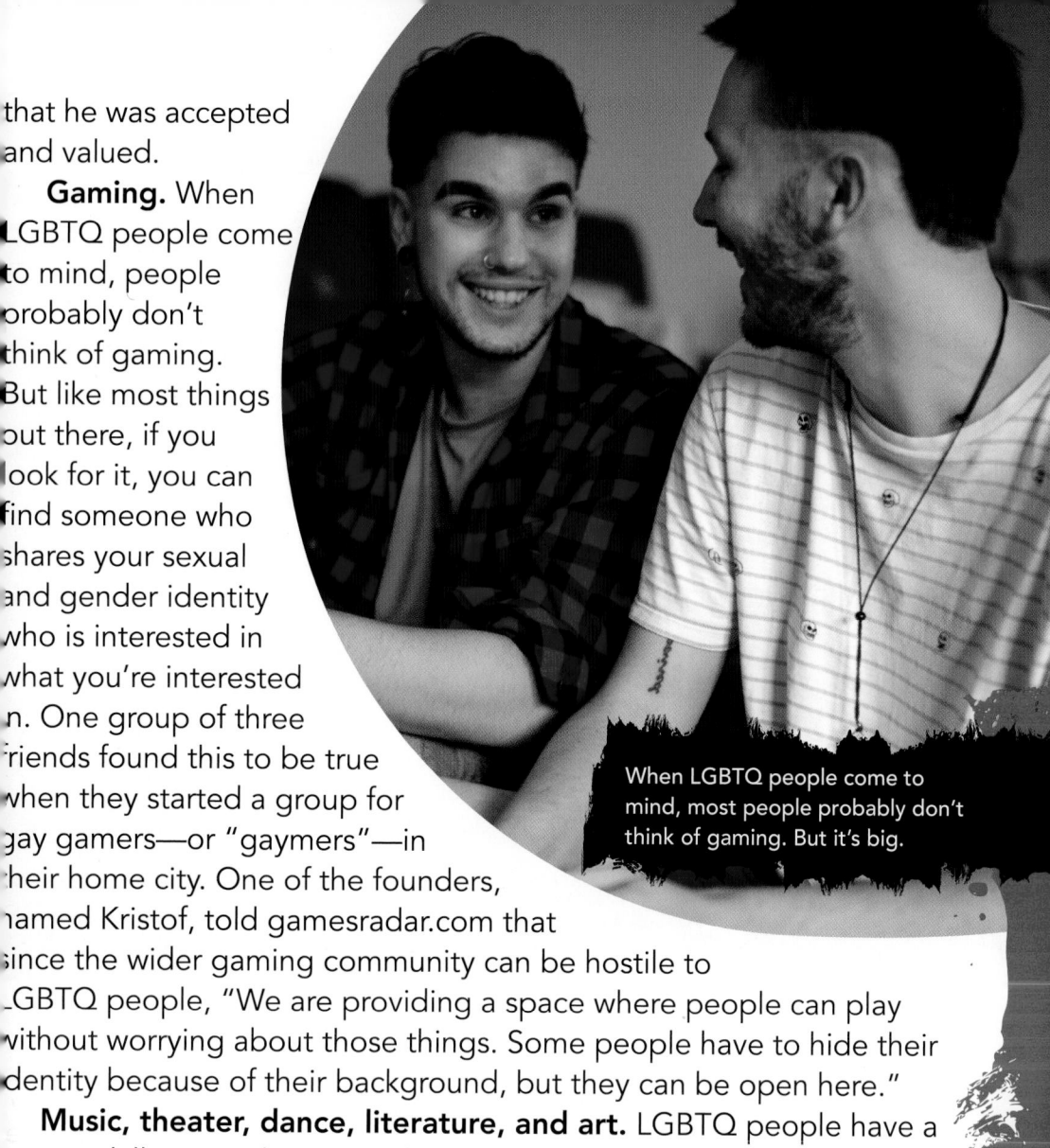

When LGBTQ people come to mind, most people probably don't think of gaming. But it's big.

Music, theater, dance, literature, and art. LGBTQ people have a long and illustrious history in the arts. Many famous artists of all types over the centuries have been members of the LGBTQ community, and there is also a long history of LGBTQ people finding each other and creating community within the context of the arts. It's an area of interest that many people within the community still share. If any of these are your interests, it may be a good way for you to find people to relate to and share your creative passion with.

Queer studies. Another interest many LGBTQ people share, unsurprisingly, is **queer studies**. This includes the study of LGBTQ

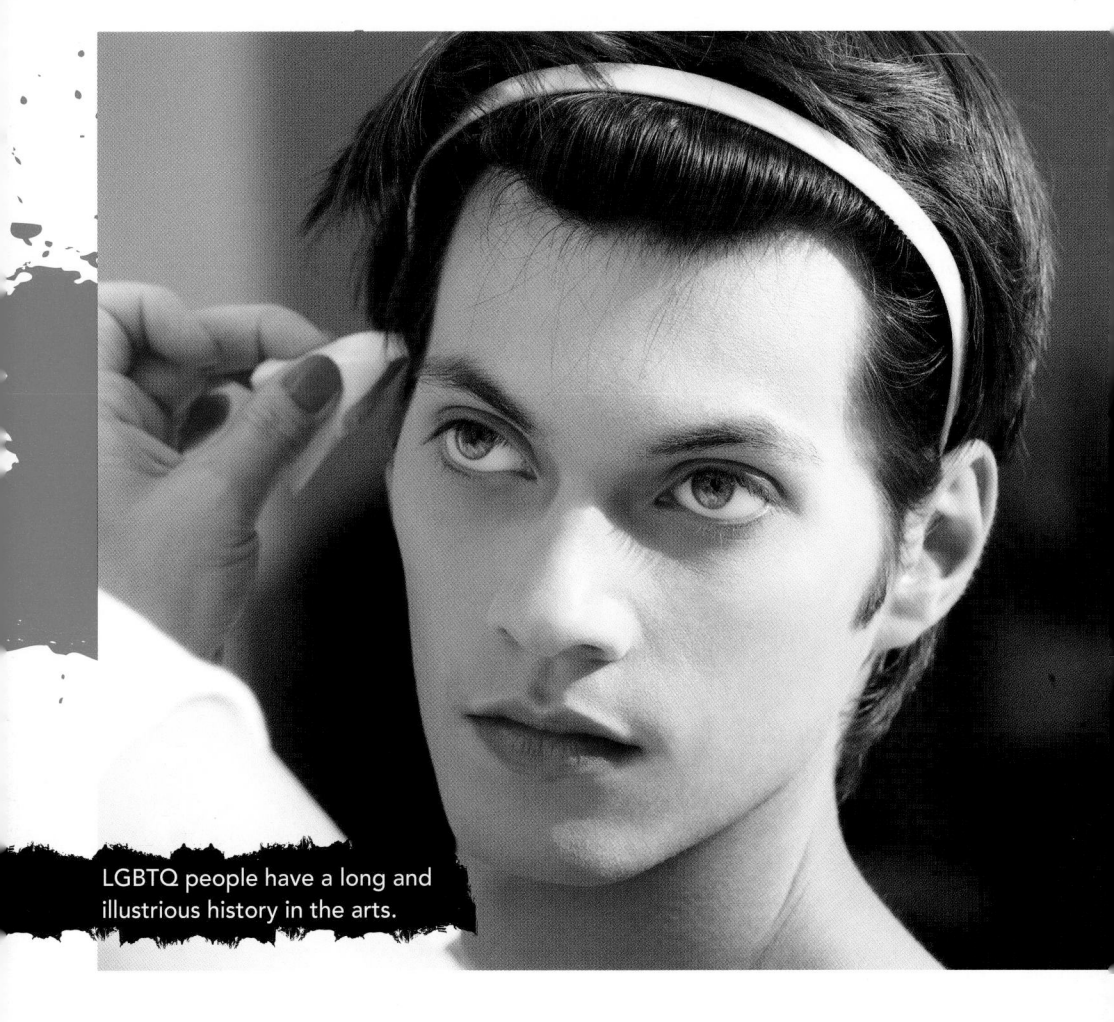

LGBTQ people have a long and illustrious history in the arts.

history but also includes anything from reading books by LGBTQ author like Audre Lorde and Gore Vidal to appreciating the photography of Robert Mapplethorpe to listening to the music of Tegan and Sara. It can also mean looking at anything else through the lens of the LGBTQ experience. If you end up going to college, you may even find a queer studies course or department at your school.

DIVERSITY IN SEXUAL AND GENDER IDENTITY

Chapter 1 should have given you an idea of the wide variety of types of people and identities under the umbrella of LGBTQ. There are a variety of other identities that people embrace to communicate even

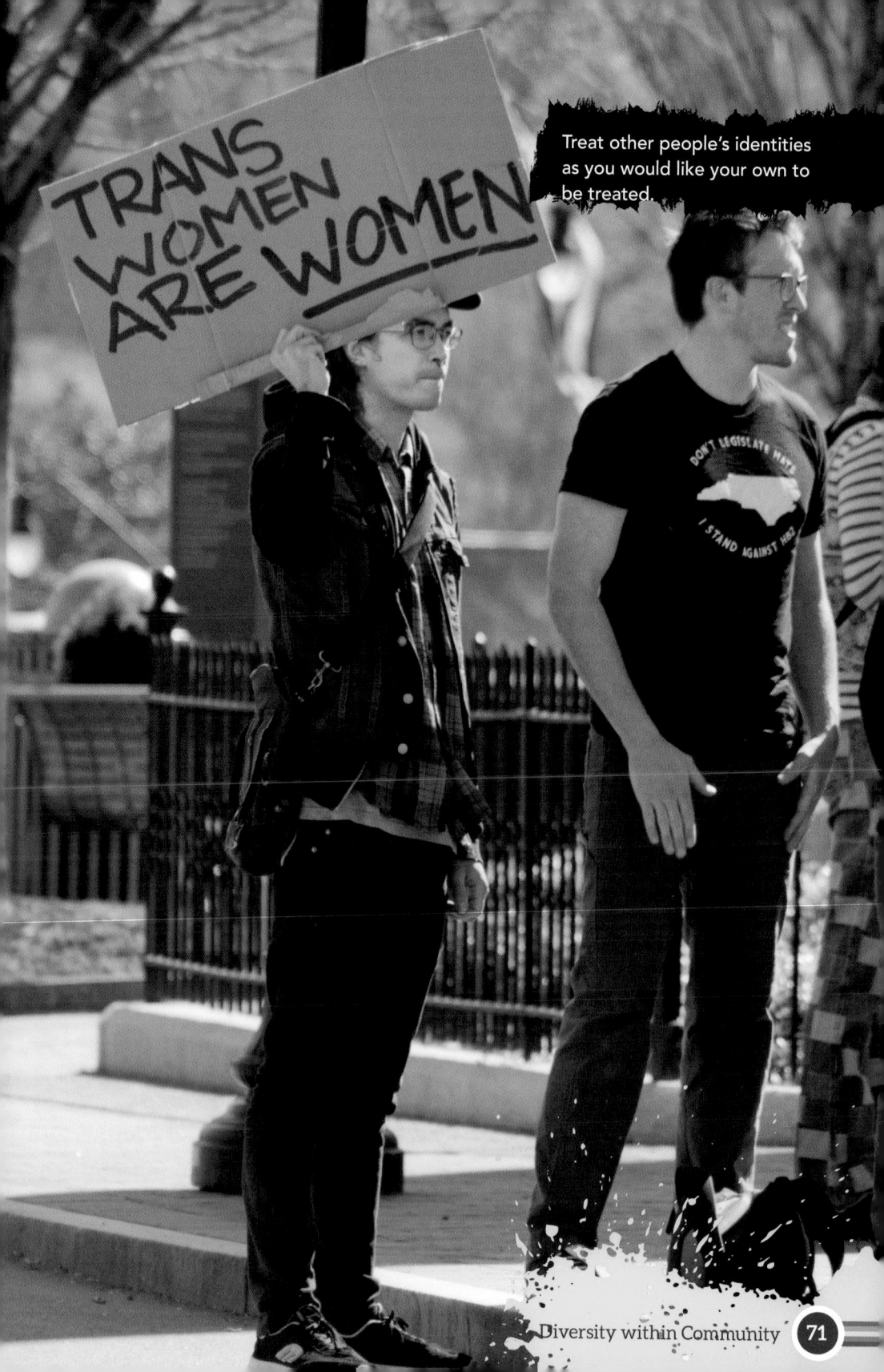

Treat other people's identities as you would like your own to be treated.

more specifically how they view themselves and how they want to present their truth about themselves to others. If someone tells you that they identify a certain way and would like you to refer to them in a certain way, you should respect that.

For some people, this means using alternate pronouns. Some examples include using *they* and *them* when referring to the person instead of *he* or *him*, or *she* or *her*, in order to be **gender-neutral**. There are other pronouns that have been created specifically for the purpose of being gender-neutral, as well. One of the more common sets of alternate pronouns used is *zie/zim/zer/zis*, used in place of the pronouns *she/her/her/hers* or *he/him/his/his*.

For others, it may mean referring to them by a name other than the one they use in situations outside the community. The golden rule always applies— treat these identities as you would like your own to be treated.

Diversity within the community is a chance to learn about those who are *not* like you.

THE BENEFITS OF DIVERSITY

The diversity within the LGBTQ community gives you an opportunity to find people who can relate to your situation and your identity. You may be able to find someone who has the same sexual orientation, gender identity, ethnicity, and similar interests. This can be a big help in making it through hard times.

But you should also use the diversity within the community as a chance to learn about those who are *not* like you. There are so many perspectives to be explored and many people who are willing to share theirs with you if you just ask. It's a chance to open your mind and understand other people's experiences—and the world—better.

Ethnicity-Specific Online Resources

National Queer Asian Pacific Islander Alliance (NQAPIA)
http://www.nqapia.org/wpp/
A federation of local organizations serving the Asian and Pacific Islander community. Check here to find a group near you.

Family Is Still Family http://familyisstillfamily.org/
Resources for Asians and Pacific Islanders who are coming out to their families or trying to understand their LGBTQ family member. Includes pamphlets translated into 25 different languages.

Black Youth Project https://byp100.org/
An organization dedicated to promoting youth advocacy and political action for black youth, including queer youth.

National Black Justice League http://nbjc.org/
A civil rights organization promoting the interests of black LGBTQ people.

Familia Es Familia https://www.familiaesfamilia.org/
Provides information for Latinx LGBTQ people and their families, including materials in Spanish.

Familia Trans Queer Liberation Movement http://familiatqlm.org/
A Latinx LGBTQ advocacy organization.

Resource for Immigrants
Immigration Equality https://www.immigrationequality.org/
An organization that provides legal help to LGBTQ immigrants, including those applying for asylum and undocumented immigrants.

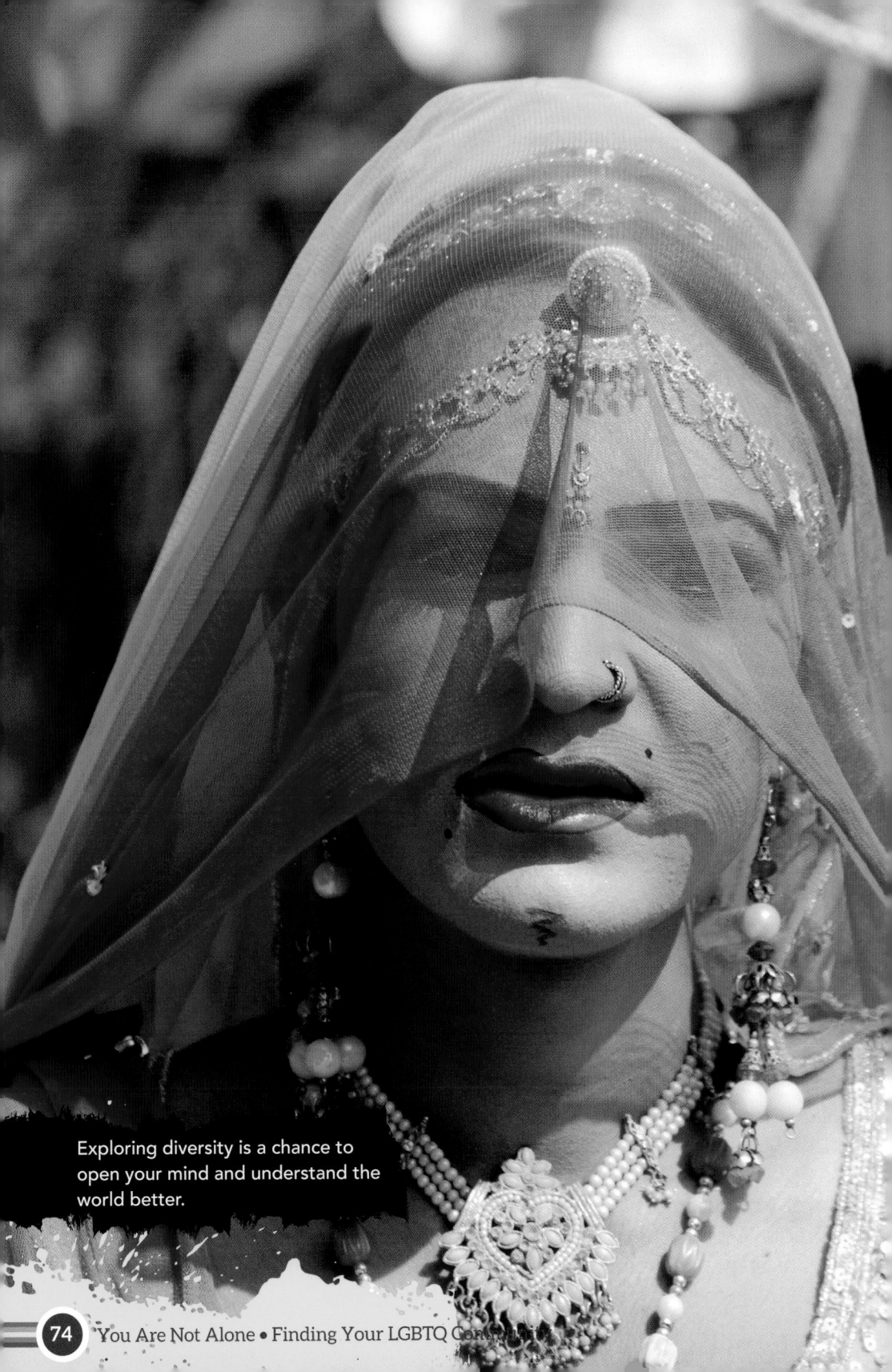

Exploring diversity is a chance to open your mind and understand the world better.

TEXT-DEPENDENT QUESTIONS

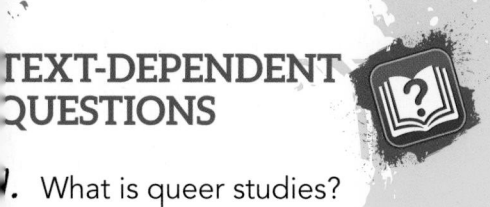

1. What is queer studies?

2. What are some of the unique challenges LGBTQ people of color face?

3. What is one way to refer to a person in a gender-neutral manner?

RESEARCH PROJECTS

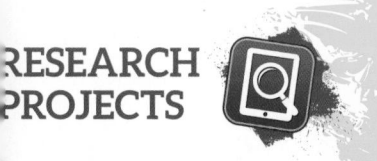

1. Think about the things that make up your identity. Write down the things about yourself that you consider the most important. These can include physical attributes, sexual/gender identity, beliefs, and interests. Do some online research on whether LGBTQ-specific groups exist for people who share that identity or interest.

2. Queer studies includes the study of all things LGBTQ. With that in mind, watch a film that you consider to be significant for LGBTQ people. Write a review of the film, including how it impacts—or makes observations about—the LGBTQ community.

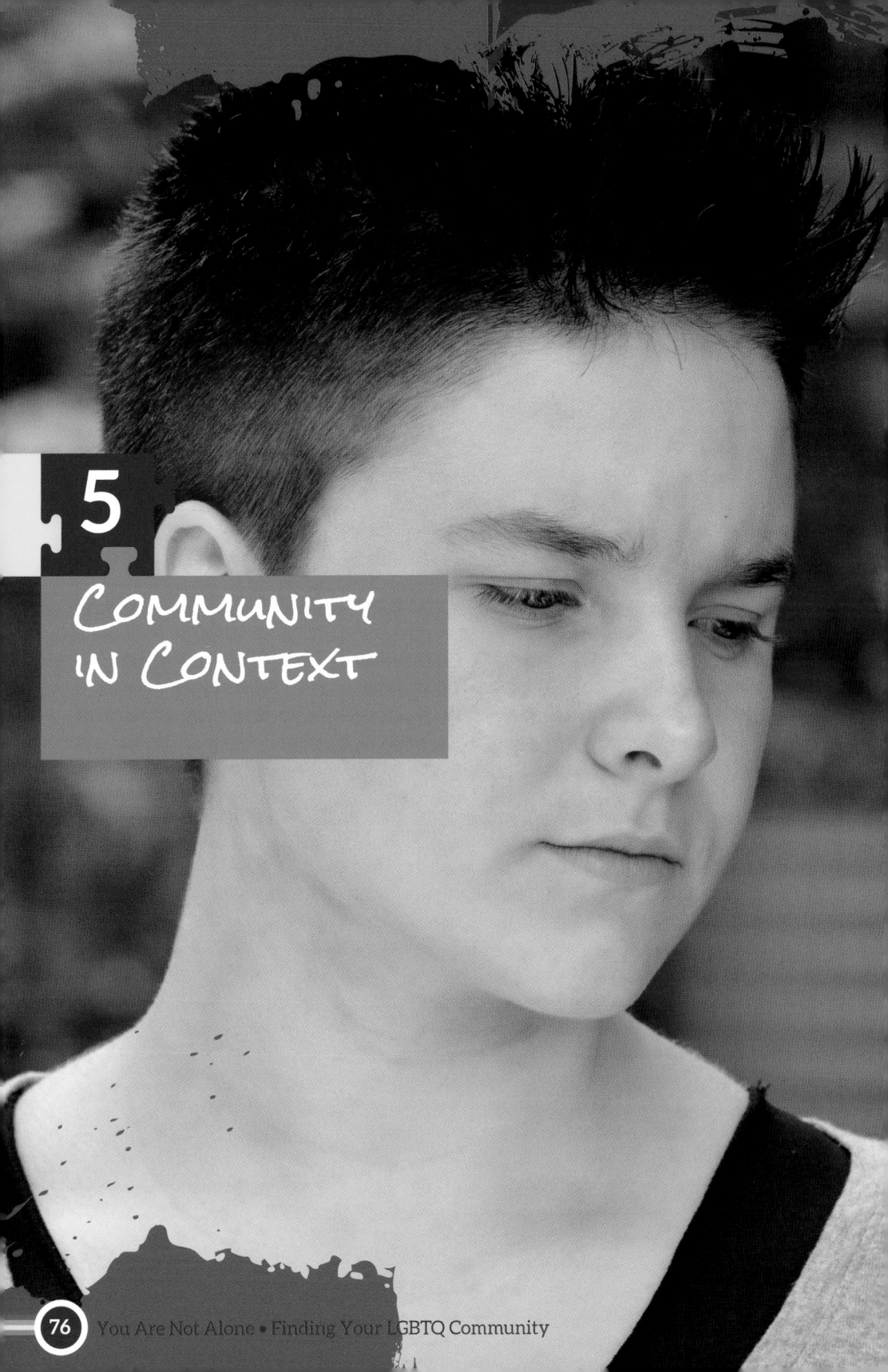

5

Community in Context

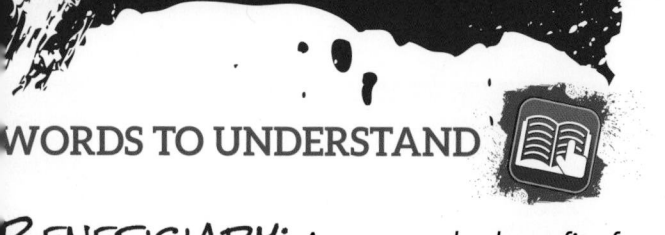

WORDS TO UNDERSTAND

BENEFICIARY: *A person who benefits from something.*

MEMORIALIZE: *To find a meaningful way to remember something or someone.*

MENTOR: *A person who is more experienced, and usually older, who advises and guides a younger, less experienced person.*

TRIBE: *A sub-category that can indicate basic attributes and personality types.*

Nick Levine spent a lot of his life feeling lonely, but he knows his was not a unique experience in that way. "Many young LGBTQ people hide their authentic selves from friends, family, and classmates before they come out, which is often an incredibly isolating experience," he wrote in the magazine *GQ*.

"This sense of isolation can be hard to shake off, and it's also easily triggered. Wherever you live in the world, however big the city, the LGBTQ community is a disparate one featuring myriad different **tribes**. It isn't always easy to find your niche. Hitting the clubs can be a euphoric experience, but it doesn't necessarily lead to long-term satisfaction. Madonna once sang, 'I found myself in crowded rooms, feeling so alone,' a sentiment many LGBTQ people can relate to."

Nick knew he needed to do something, to change something to overcome his loneliness. "Things finally got better when I was in my late twenties. By this time, I was living in London and meeting people from different backgrounds and different parts of the world. Moving to a bigger city has been the best thing for me. For the first time, I've been able to form a good group of gay friends and create my own support network. I always thought finding a boyfriend would be a life-changer for me, but it was actually finding people on the same level as me, people with common interests." Many people are

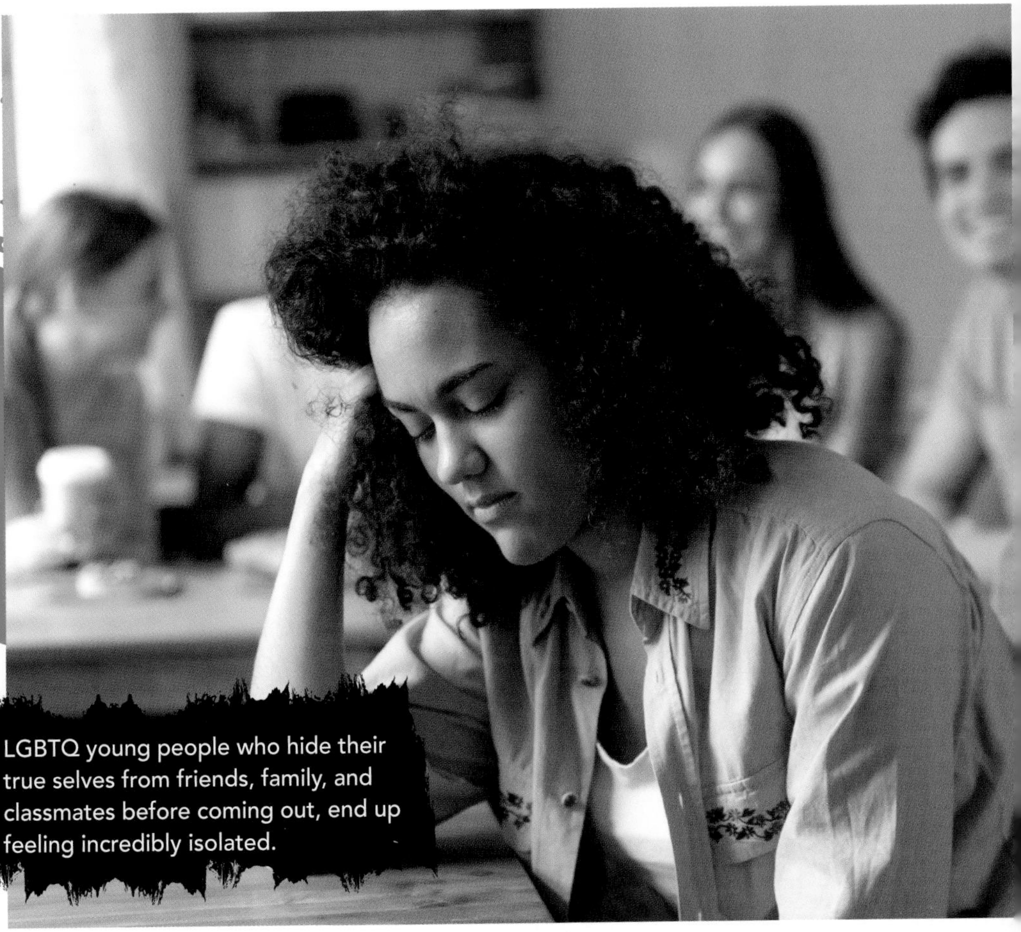

LGBTQ young people who hide their true selves from friends, family, and classmates before coming out, end up feeling incredibly isolated.

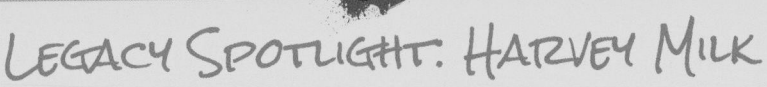

Legacy Spotlight: Harvey Milk

One of the most famous and influential figures in LGBTQ civil rights history, Harvey Milk was an activist and politician in San Francisco in the 1970s. He was the first openly gay elected politician in the United States having been elected to the San Francisco Board of Supervisors.

In 1978, Milk was assassinated along with the mayor of San Francisco, George Moscone, in city hall by an anti-gay member of the Board of Supervisors. Ever since then, Milk's name has been a rallying cry for the LGBTQ rights movement, particularly in San Francisco.

Milk was depicted in the film *Milk* by Sean Penn and is the subject of the documentary *The Times of Harvey Milk*.

HARVEY MILK

Harvey Milk was one of the most influential figures in LGBTQ civil rights history,

FOREVER US

able to find community while in their youth, but for others it is the opportunities that become open to them as adults that provide them with community.

PHASES OF LIFE

As time goes by, and your life situation changes, you will find your community changing as well. When you graduate from school—and move on from your GSA if you have one—you may find a similar organization at college (should you choose to go). You may keep in touch with your friends and support system from high school, or you may find yourself drawn to a new group of people. The important thing is, as you get older, your community may change, and that's okay.

A lot changes when you turn 18. As an adult, you're able to make more decisions for yourself. You can choose to stay where you are and form a community there, or you can choose to move to a new place and find a new one. Some other options to meet people open up for you when you become an adult. A lot of LGBTQ social media content is aimed at adults, much of which you can't access until you are at least 18. Some clubs have 18-and-up dance parties

A lot of LGBTQ social spaces are only open to people 21 and up.

and events at certain times, which can be a great way to meet new people.

When you turn 21, a new set of opportunities open for you. Unfortunately, a lot of LGBTQ social spaces are only open to people 21 and up. These include most places that serve alcohol, like bars, clubs, and even some restaurants. Once you're able to go, these spaces can create more opportunities to meet people and form community.

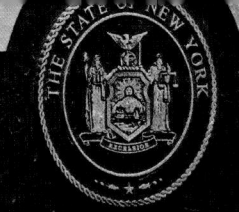

The Stonewall Inn

The events that began at the Stonewall Inn in 1969 marked a monumental change for lesbian, gay, bisexual, transgender and queer (LGBTQ) Americans. Stonewall, which occupied 51-53 Christopher Street, was a gay bar that was raided on June 28, 1969. Patrons and a crowd outside resisted, and confrontations continued over the next few nights in nearby Christopher Park and on adjacent streets. This uprising catalyzed the LGBTQ civil rights movement, resulting in increased visibility for the community that continues to resonate in the struggle for equality.

New York State Historic Site
2016

The Stonewall Inn, where the modern LGBTQ rights movement began, was designated a landmark in 2016.

LEGACY SPOTLIGHT: MARSHA P. JOHNSON

Marsha P. Johnson was a prominent activist and community fixture in Greenwich Village in New York City from the 1960s to 1990s. She was famously an important part of the Stonewall Riots at the Stonewall Inn bar in 1969, an event that is often credited as kicking off the LGBTQ rights movement.

Marsha also helped form a service organization called S.T.A.R.—Street Transvestite Action Revolutionaries. (*Transgender* was not a commonly used term at the time). She was known as a beloved mentor to drag queens and other gender-non-conforming young people.

Legacy Spotlight: Sylvia Rivera

A friend of Marsha P. Johnson's, Sylvia participated in the 1969 Stonewall Riots and was a co-founder of S.T.A.R. with Marsha. Sylvia was also a founding member of the Gay Liberation Front and the Gay Activist Alliance, two radical LGBTQ rights organizations in New York City.

As a woman of Puerto Rican and Venezuelan descent, she was especially active in trying to help queer youth of color among New York City's homeless population. She is often referred to as a transgender activist, though she at times rejected all labels.

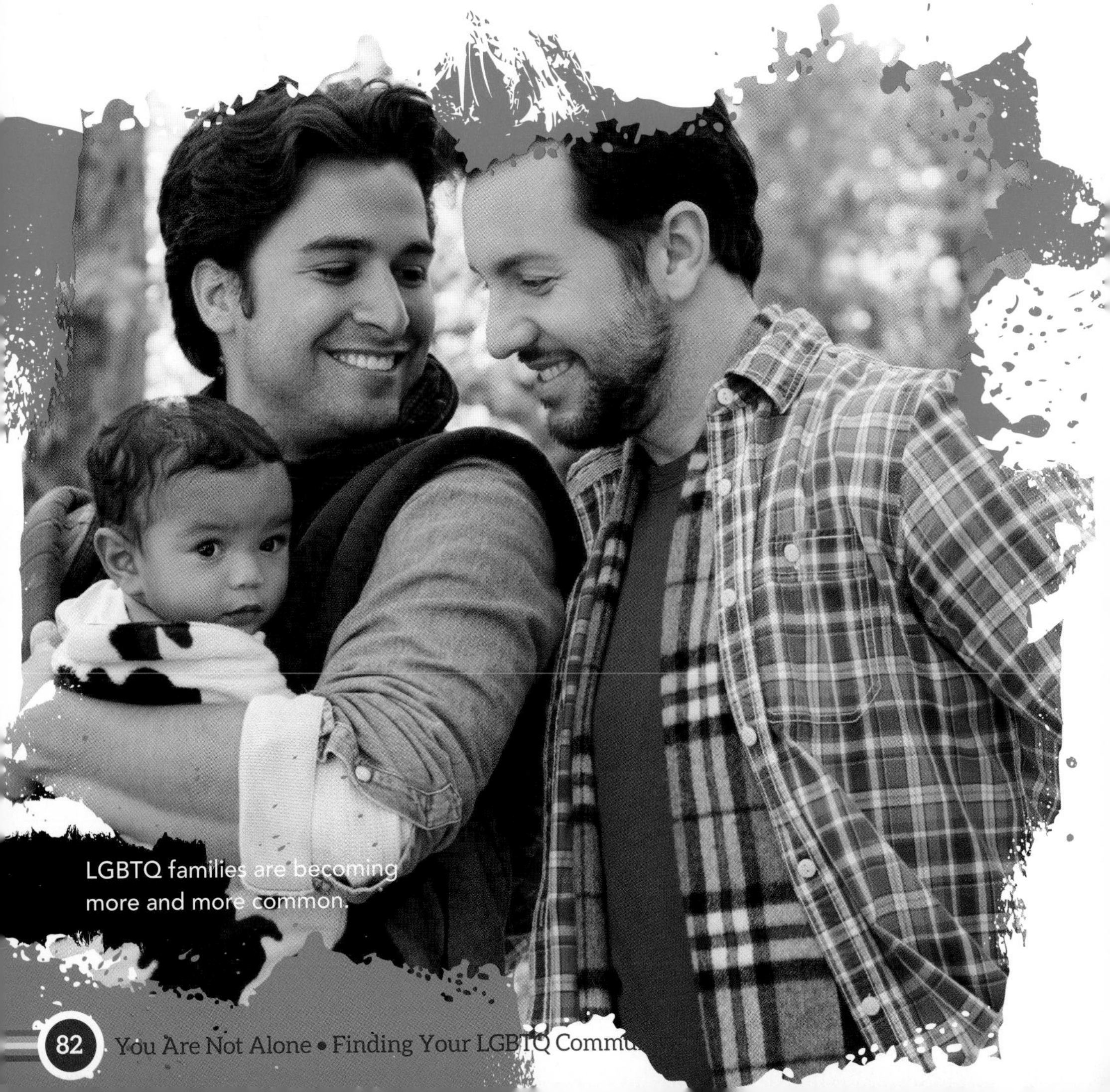

LGBTQ families are becoming more and more common.

FAMILY

A person's lifestyle options increase as they enter adulthood as well. It used to be assumed that LGBTQ people wouldn't create families of their own, but that's no longer the case. LGBTQ families are becoming more and more common. Same-sex marriage has brought more acceptance and legal protection for many LGBTQ couples and families. Adoption agencies are more interested in placing children with same-sex couples than ever before. Surrogacy—when a woman carries a child for someone else—and artificial insemination—when a woman is impregnated without having sex with a man—is an option for many families. If you want a family, you can have one! Or, as HRC puts it, "Some people talk as if there are two options in life: You can marry someone of the opposite sex and become a family, or you can be LGBT and be excluded from the definition of family. This is patently untrue." For some people, their family becomes the most important part of their personal community. Being with their partner and their children is what makes them feel supported and comfortable.

If this isn't what you want, or it doesn't work for you, that's okay too. Many LGBTQ people have lived—and do live—full, happy lives as single persons. Often, these people create a chosen family, people they have close, strong relationships with, without having a biological bond to them.

LEGACY SPOTLIGHT: DEL MARTIN AND PHYLLIS LYON

Along with six other women, Del Martin and Phyllis Lyon were founding members of the Daughters of Bilitis, the first civil rights organization for lesbians in the United States In 1955, the Daughters of Bilitis began meeting, and by the next year, they had begun to distribute a publication called *The Ladder*. Soon, there were chapters of the organization all over the country.

Much later in life, after decades of political activism, Del and Phyllis were one of the first same-sex couples to be legally married in California, after having been together for over 50 years. Just two months after finally being able to marry her wife, Del passed away.

FINDING YOUR NICHE

As an adult, it also becomes easier to find other people with the interests discussed in the last chapter and people who are similar to you in other ways. There are many subsets of LGBTQ people whom you may encounter and find yourself drawn to. Some of these subsets are referred to as *tribes*. For example, the two most common tribe nicknames for gay men are *twink* and *bear*. *Twink* refers to young, small guys. *Bear* refers to bigger, older guys with body hair. Those are just two of the many tribe names to choose from. These types of group nicknames are generally used playfully but can be used to find others you can feel like you fit in—or maybe to find people you're attracted to.

For Swen Nielsen, from Salt Lake City, Utah, finding his niche as an adult meant joining sports leagues meant specifically for LGBTQ people and allies. "When I was ready and looking to find friends within our community, I knew I had to have common interest. Loving and playing sports as much as I do, I hoped that would be my outlet. I was very lucky to find that the area of Salt Lake City has an LGBTQ swim team. I started there and found so many friends both LGBTQ and straight. I learned of all the opportunities there are out there to get me involved in our community. So I got involved,

Bayard Rustin was a lifelong political activist and a close associate of Dr. Martin Luther King Jr.

Sally Ride

Bayard Rustin

I competed, I coached, I mentored. There is so much to be thankful for. It's amazing knowing that I can be myself and do what I love."

GETTING INVOLVED

Just as when you're young, when you're an adult, there are many other ways to be involved. As Swen mentioned, in addition to participating in sports, he helped others get involved and worked as a **mentor** with them. Mentoring means helping people who are younger or less experienced in something, which can include helping those who are still underage find their own place in the community. Just as you benefit from community now while you are in school, you can help others feel those same benefits by giving back when you are able.

Other types of volunteering include political activism, volunteering at a community center, participating in college campus organizations, volunteering with health services such as HIV testing, helping care for the LGBTQ elderly, and so many others. Of course, it's always great to volunteer outside of the LGBTQ community as well, and you'll be surprised at the community you can find there.

Working with LGBTQ elderly can be an especially great way to discover the diversity of experience within the LGBTQ community. Hearing an older person's stories of struggle, survival, love, sadness,

LEGACY SPOTLIGHT: BAYARD RUSTIN

Bayard Rustin was a lifelong political activist for many different causes, from labor organizing to pacifism to LGBTQ rights. He is most well-known for being a close associate of Dr. Martin Luther King Jr. and having organized the March on Washington that included Dr. King's "I Have a Dream" speech.

Bayard was always open about his sexuality while working in the civil rights movement, even though it meant that he could not be a prominent spokesperson for the movement. Later in life, he argued that the gay rights movement had become the standard by which a person could measure the progress of society.

and happiness can give you insights into the queer experience that you can't get anywhere else. Find someone who is willing to talk to you, ask them as many questions as you can, and prepare to have your mind blown. There are service organizations that cater specifically to helping elderly LGBTQ people—there are even some retirement homes now, just for LGBTQ people.

THE LEGACY OF THE LBGTQ COMMUNITY

Because of the members of the community who came before, LGBTQ people now can live openly.

The LGBTQ community has a history to be proud of. It includes struggle, pain, hardship, and even a significant amount of death. But there have also been a lot of victories, a lot of joy, and a lot of love. Because of the members of the community who came before, LGBTQ people now can live openly, loving whom they choose, and marrying, and they can do these things proudly and publicly.

If you are an LGBTQ person, you are a part of that legacy. If you are LGBTQ,

Bridging the Queer Age Gap: LGBTQ + Ice Cream Social
Chosen Family: Stories of Queer Resilience

you are a **beneficiary** of it. And you have the opportunity to pick up that torch and run with it so that those who come after you can say they are beneficiaries of what you did.

YOUR PLACE IN THE COMMUNITY

Hopefully, this book has shown you that you have a place in the community. No matter what your sexual orientation, gender identity, race, interests, personality, strengths, weaknesses, talents, or flaws are, you will be welcomed somewhere in the LGBTQ community. The community is not

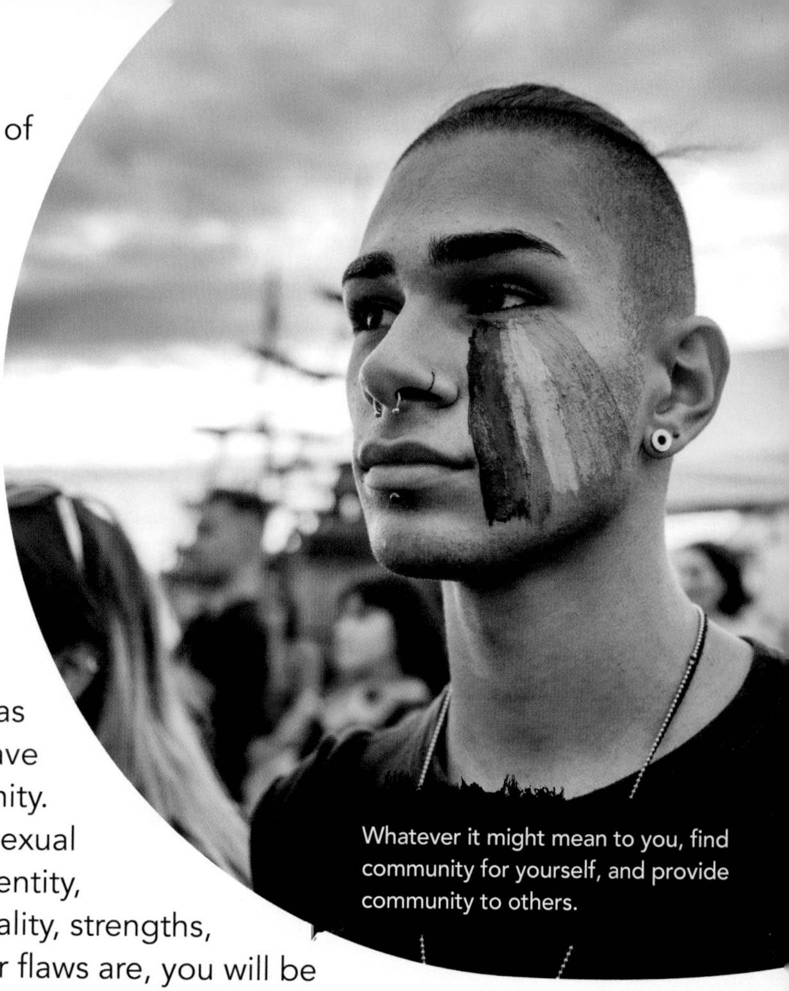

Whatever it might mean to you, find community for yourself, and provide community to others.

LEGACY SPOTLIGHT: CLEVE JONES

One of the great living legends of the LGBTQ rights movement, Cleve Jones, was instrumental in creating the community as it exists today. In the 1970s, he worked with Harvey Milk in San Francisco on gay civil rights issues.

Later, during the AIDS crisis, Cleve was a leading advocate for AIDS patients. He helped create the AIDS Memorial Quilt, which brought national attention to the crisis. Each panel of the quilt represents one victim of the disease whom a loved one wanted to memorialize. There are now over 40,000 panels in the quilt.

Cleve was depicted as a character in both the film *Milk* and the TV miniseries *When We Rise*.

perfect, and you might not immediately find your niche or your corner of the LGBTQ world. But it is out there, and if you are persistent, you can find it.

Know that there are people who have experienced what you are going through and who have come out on the other side a healthy, happy person. And there are people who have done that and are willing to help you do the same. If you are one of the people who has already come out on the other side, remember that there are LGBTQ people who are struggling and could use your help.

That's what being a community means: being there for each other when you are in need, and supporting each other in your struggles. And yes, community also means spending time together, having fun, and celebrating what it means to be LGBTQ. It can mean marching in Pride parades or going out with friends. Community can even mean finding a special someone to support you and make you feel accepted for the rest of your life.

Whatever it might mean to you, find community for yourself, and provide community to others.

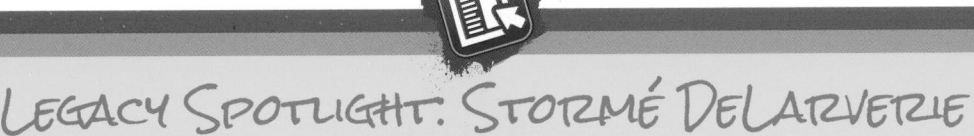

LEGACY SPOTLIGHT: STORMÉ DELARVERIE

Stormé was an entertainer in New York City in the second half of the 20th century, performing as a singer and emcee at many venues, including the Apollo Theater. According to some versions of the Stonewall Riots story (there is some confusion as to how it all played out), it was Stormé's arrest and challenge to the crowd to come to her assistance that started the riot. She also worked as a bouncer at many of the lesbian bars in NYC and was known to patrol the neighborhood on her own to defend other lesbians against harassment.

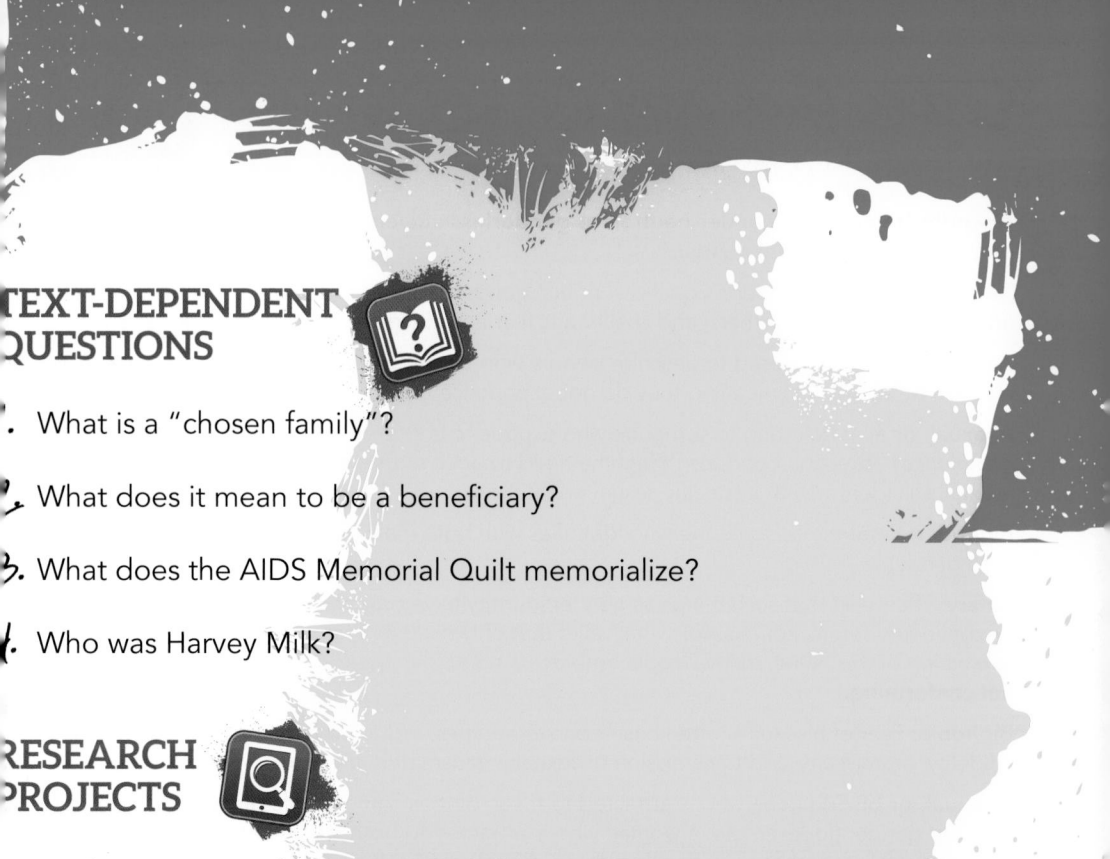

TEXT-DEPENDENT QUESTIONS

1. What is a "chosen family"?

2. What does it mean to be a beneficiary?

3. What does the AIDS Memorial Quilt memorialize?

4. Who was Harvey Milk?

RESEARCH PROJECTS

1. Find a prominent figure in LGBTQ history. Write a short biography of that person. What did they do that was significant? How was life different for them than it is now? How does what they did affect the modern LGBTQ community or you personally?

2. Think deeply, and write out your thoughts: What does community look like to you? What would make you feel supported? How might you be able to find that kind of community now or sometime in the future?

Agender (or neutrois, gender neutral, or genderless): Referring to someone who has little or no personal connection with gender.

Ally: Someone who supports equal civil rights, gender equality, and LGBTQ social movements; advocates on behalf of others; and challenges fear and discrimination in all its forms.

Asexual: An adjective used to describe people who do not experience sexual attraction. A person can also be aromantic, meaning they do not experience romantic attraction.

Asexual, or ace: Referring to someone who experiences little or no sexual attraction, or who experiences attraction but doesn't feel the need to act it out sexually. Many people who are asexual still identify with a specific sexual orientation.

Bigender: Referring to someone who identifies with both male and female genders, or even a third gender.

Binary: The belief that such things as gender identity have only two distinct, opposite, and disconnected forms. For example, the belief that only male and female genders exist. As a rejection of this belief, many people embrace a non-binary gender identity. (See **Gender nonconforming.**)

Biphobia: Fear of bisexuals, often based on stereotypes, including inaccurate associations with infidelity, promiscuity, and transmission of sexually transmitted infections.

Bisexual, or bi: Someone who is attracted to those of their same gender as well as to those of a different gender (for example, a woman who is attracted to both women and men). Some people use the word bisexual as an umbrella term to describe individuals that are attracted to more than one gender. In this way, the term is closely related to pansexual, or omnisexual, meaning someone who is attracted to people of any gender identity.

Butch, or masc: Someone whose gender expression is masculine. *Butch* is sometimes used as a derogatory term for lesbians, but it can also be claimed as an affirmative identity label.

Cisgender, or cis: A person whose gender identity matches the gender they were assigned at birth.

Coming out: The process through which a person accepts their sexual orientation and/or gender identity as part of their overall identity. For many, this involves sharing that identity with others, which makes it more of a lifetime process rather than just a one-time experience.

Cross-dresser: While anyone may wear clothes associated with a different sex, the term is typically used to refer to men who occasionally wear clothes, makeup, and accessories that are culturally associated with women. Those men typically identify as heterosexual. This activity is a form of gender expression and not done for entertainment purposes. Cross-dressers do not wish to permanently change their sex or live full-time as women.

Drag: The act of presenting as a different gender, usually for the purpose of entertainment (i.e., drag kings and queens). Many people who do drag do not wish to present as a different gender all of the time.

Gay: Someone who is attracted to those of their same gender. This is often used as an umbrella term but is used more specifically to describe men who are attracted to men.

Gender affirmation surgery: Medical procedures that some individuals elect to undergo to change their physical appearance to resemble more closely the way they view their gender identity.

Gender expression: The external manifestations of gender, expressed through such things as names, pronouns, clothing, haircuts, behavior, voice, and body characteristics.

Gender identity: One's internal, deeply held sense of gender. Some people identify completely with the gender they were assigned at birth (usually male or female), while others may identify with only a part of that gender or not at all. Some people identify with another gender entirely. Unlike gender expression, gender identity is not visible to others.

Gender nonconforming: Referring to someone whose gender identity and/or gender expression does not conform to the cultural or social expectations of gender, particularly in relation to male or female. This can be an umbrella term for many identities, including, but not limited to:

> **Genderfluid:** Someone whose gender identity and/or expression varies over time.

> **Genderqueer (or third gender):** Someone whose gender identity and/or expression falls between or outside of male and female.

Heterosexual: An adjective used to describe people whose enduring physical, romantic, and/ or emotional attraction is to people of the opposite sex. Also **straight**.

Homophobia: Fear of people who are attracted to the same sex. *Intolerance*, *bias*, or *prejudice* are usually more accurate descriptions of antipathy toward LGBTQ people.

Intergender: Referring to someone whose identity is between genders and/or a combination of gender identities and expressions.

Intersectionality: The idea that multiple identities intersect to create a whole that is different from its distinct parts. To understand someone, it is important to acknowledge that each of their identities is important and inextricably linked with all of the others. These can include identities related to gender, race, socioeconomic status, ethnicity, nationality, sexual orientation, religion, age, mental and/or physical ability, and more.

Intersex: Referring to someone who, due to a variety of factors, has reproductive or sexual anatomy that does not seem to fit the typical definitions for the female or male sex. Some people who are intersex may identify with the gender assigned to them at birth, while many others do not.

Lesbian: A woman who is attracted to other women. Some lesbians prefer to identify as gay women.

LGBTQ: Acronym for lesbian, gay, bisexual, transgender, and queer or questioning.

Non-binary and/or genderqueer: Terms used by some people who experience their gender identity and/or gender expression as falling outside the categories of man and woman. They may define their gender as falling somewhere in between man and woman, or they may define it as wholly different from these terms.

Out: Referring to a person who self-identifies as LGBTQ in their personal, public, and/or professional lives.

Pangender: Referring to a person whose identity comprises all or many gender identities and expressions.

Pride: The celebration of LGBTQ identities and the global LGBTQ community's resistance against discrimination and violence. Pride events are celebrated in many countries around the world, usually during the month of June to commemorate the Stonewall Riots that began in New York City in June 1969, a pivotal moment in the modern LGBTQ movement.

Queer: An adjective used by some people, particularly younger people, whose sexual orientation is not exclusively heterosexual (e.g., queer person, queer woman). Typically, for those who identify as queer, the terms *lesbian*, *gay*, and *bisexual* are perceived to be too limiting and/or fraught with cultural connotations that they feel don't apply to them. Some people may use *queer*, or

more commonly *genderqueer*, to describe their gender identity and/or gender expression (see **non-binary** and/or **genderqueer**). Once considered a pejorative term, *queer* has been reclaimed by some LGBT people to describe themselves; however, it is not a universally accepted term, even within the LGBT community. When Q is seen at the end of LGBT, it may mean *queer* or *questioning*.

Questioning: A time in many people's lives when they question or experiment with their gender expression, gender identity, and/or sexual orientation. This experience is unique to everyone; for some, it can last a lifetime or be repeated many times over the course of a lifetime.

Sex: At birth, infants are commonly assigned a sex. This is usually based on the appearance of their external anatomy and is often confused with gender. However, a person's sex is actually a combination of bodily characteristics including chromosomes, hormones, internal and external reproductive organs, and secondary sex characteristics. As a result, there are many more sexes than just the binary male and female, just as there are many more genders than just male and female.

Sex reassignment surgery: See **Gender affirmation surgery**.

Sexual orientation: A person's enduring physical, romantic, and/or emotional attraction to another person. Gender identity and sexual orientation are not the same. Transgender people may be straight, lesbian, gay, bisexual, or queer. For example, a person who transitions from male to female and is attracted solely to men would typically identify as a straight woman.

Straight, or heterosexual: A word to describe women who are attracted to men and men who are attracted to women. This is not exclusive to those who are cisgender. For example, transgender men may identify as straight because they are attracted to women.

They/Them/Their: One of many sets of gender-neutral singular pronouns in English that can be used as an alternative to he/him/his or she/her/hers. Usage of this particular set is becoming increasingly prevalent, particularly within the LGBTQ community.

Transgender: An umbrella term for people whose gender identity and/or gender expression differs from what is typically associated with the sex they were assigned at birth. People under the transgender umbrella may describe themselves using one or more of a wide variety of terms—including transgender. A transgender identity is not dependent upon physical appearance or medical procedures.

Transgender man: People who were assigned female at birth but identify and live as a man may use this term to describe themselves. They may shorten it to *trans man*. Some may also use *FTM*, an abbreviation for *female-to-male*. Some may prefer to simply be called *men*, without any modifier. It is best to ask which term a person prefers.

Transgender woman: People who were assigned male at birth but identify and live as a woman may use this term to describe themselves. They may shorten it to *trans woman*. Some may also use *MTF*, an abbreviation for *male-to-female*. Some may prefer to simply be called *female*, without any modifier.

Transition: Altering one's birth sex is not a one-step procedure; it is a complex process that occurs over a long period of time. Transition can include some or all of the following personal, medical, and legal steps: telling one's family, friends, and co-workers; using a different name and new pronouns; dressing differently; changing one's name and/or sex on legal documents; hormone therapy; and possibly (though not always) one or more types of surgery. The exact steps involved in transition vary from person to person.

Transsexual: Someone who has undergone, or wishes to undergo, gender affirmation surgery. This is an older term that originated in the medical and psychological communities. Although many transgender people do not identify as transsexual, some still prefer the term.

Further Reading & Internet Resources

BOOKS

Langford, Jo. *The Pride Guide: A Guide to Sexual and Social Health for LGBTQ Youth*. London: Rowman and Littlefield, 2018.

Few LGBTQ youth receive sex education in schools that address the issues specific to them. This book seeks to fill that gap, giving teens the information they need, at their level, without talking down to them. Beyond sex ed., though, the book provides information for navigating life as a young LGBTQ person.

Mardell, Ashley. *The ABC's of LGBT+*. Mango Media, Inc., 2016.

A comprehensive but conversational introduction to what it means to be LGBTQ. It includes a "cheat sheet" of relevant terms and an overview of concepts like sexual and gender identity.

Newton, David E. *LGBT Youth Issues Today: A Reference Handbook (Contemporary World Issues)*. Denver, Colorado: ABC-CLIO, 2014.

An extensive overview of the issues facing young LGBTQ people, including societal and family acceptance, homelessness, depression, and suicide. It also gives an introduction to LGBTQ history and resources for helping those around you to understand what being LGBTQ means.

WEB SITES

GSA Network. www.gsanetwork.com
The Genders and Sexualities Alliance Network provides resources to local GSA clubs in creating LGBTQ community for students at middle schools and high schools. GSA chapters are now in schools throughout the country.

Human Rights Campaign. www.hrc.org
As the largest LGBTQ organization in the country, HRC has advocated for the rights of sexual and gender minorities at every level of government since 1980. In addition to political work, HRC also conducts advocacy and education initiatives within local communities. The Web site includes resources for LGBTQ people and those trying to understand them.

GLSEN. www.glsen.org
Pronounced "glisten." An organization founded by teachers for the purpose of helping LGBTQ youth in the context of education. It works to make schools as safe and LGBTQ-friendly as possible.

It Gets Better Project. www.itgetsbetter.org
The It Gets Better Project began in 2010, when Dan Savage and Terry Miller uploaded a video to YouTube, meant to give young LGBTQ people hope for the future. Since then, more than 60,000 people have shared their stories, as well as words of inspiration and encouragement, all of which can be viewed on their Web site.

The Trevor Project. www.thetrevorproject.org
A suicide prevention and mental health resource specifically for LGBTQ youth. The Trevor Project provides counseling over the phone and through chat online.

PFLAG. www.pflag.org
Parents and Friends of Lesbians and Gays. The largest organization for allies of LGBTQ people in the country, providing resources to parents and loved ones.

CenterLink—The Community of LGBT Centers. www.lgbtcenters.org
An organization that ties together LGBTQ community centers across the country. The Web site includes a directory of centers.

Author's Biography

Jeremy Quist is a writer and California native. He conducted academic research on LGBTQ identity and community in Eastern Europe and wrote about his experiences at www.we2boys.com. He's lived throughout the Western United States and now splits his time between Northern California and the road.

Credits

COVER

(clockwise from top left) iStock/SoumenNath; iStock/Rawpixel; iStock/Rawpixel; iStock/Rawpixel;

INTERIOR